GRIZZL

CAUTIONARY TALES FOR LOVERS OF SQUEAM

superZeroes

IS IT A BIRD?
IS IT A PLANE?

NO. IT'S A STUPID READER-CHILD SLEEPWALKING INTO A WHOLE BIG BOOK OF BEWARES!

Also in this series:

GRIZZLY TALES

'CAUTIONARY TALES FOR LOVERS OF SQUEAM'

superZeroes

JAMIE RIX
Illustrated by Steven Pattison

CLOSE THE COVER BEFORE YOU'RE IN TOO DEEP.

Orion
Children's Books

Behind this door is the SS *Pain and Everlasting Torment*. This porthole is all that stands between you and permanent doomage! Enter and you will never return! Do you want the captain to lock you up in Davy Jones Locker?

For Carina, Jessica and Zoe

First published in Great Britain in 2008
by Orion Children's Books
a division of the Orion Publishing Group Ltd
Orion House
5 Upper St Martin's Lane
London WC2H 9EA
An Hachette Livre company

1 3 5 7 9 10 8 6 4 2

A catalogue record for this book is available from the British Library.

Printed in Great Britain

ISBN 978 1 84255 648 1

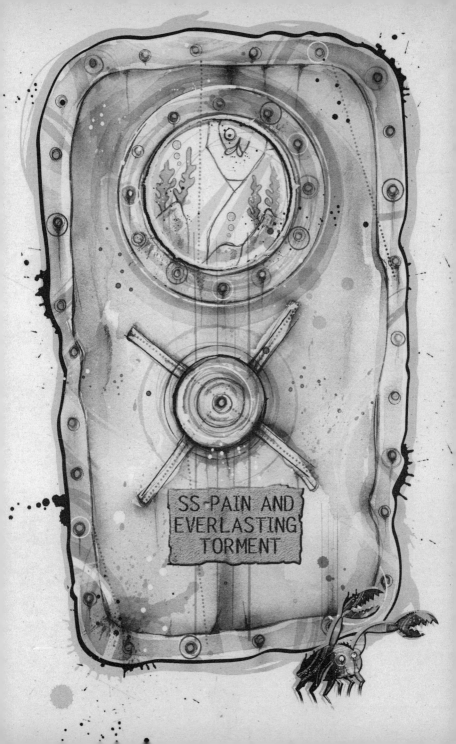

To avoid a lashing from the Cat O'Nine Tails and certain death after Walking the Plank into the gaping jaws of a crocodile, take the following simple precautions.

1. Make a lifelike puppet of a British Bulldog out of an old sock. Keep it in your pocket. When the Captain produces the Cat O'Nine Tails, produce your sock puppet and watch the cat run away with its nine tails between its legs!

2. Use this clever SPLINTER ME FOOT KIT, containing three ready-to-use, pre-sharpened wooden splinters. Simply push a splinter into the sole of your foot. Then wait until you are halfway down the plank when you should suddenly cry out, clutch your foot and hop up and down in mock pain.* The key to a successful use of the SPLINTER ME FOOT KIT is to pretend that you got the splinter from the plank. With cries such as, 'Ooh my foot!' and 'I can't go on. It really hurts!' the evil Captain will immediately take pity on you (because even evil Captains know how sore splinters can be) and send you down to Sick Bay to have the splinter removed. Once in Sick Bay you can mount an escape by paralysing everyone on board with a hypodermic needle and stealing a life boat.

The British Bulldog Sock Puppet (note its lifelike features).

*Take care not to fall off the sides of the plank obviously, because this would rather defeat the point of the SPLINTER ME FOOT KIT.

The SS *Pain and Everlasting Torment*
We take the Naughty out of Naughtical!

Welcome Aboard!
Your Captain Needs YOU!

TODAY'S EVENTS

SCRUBBING THE POOP DECK SOMEONE HAS TO SCRUB THE FISH POOP OFF THE DECK AND THAT SOMEONE IS YOU! I DON'T DO POOP SCRUBBING. STARTS 6.00 HRS TILL LATE. BRING A TOOTHBRUSH TO SCRUB WITH.

SPLICING THE MAIN BRACE - TRADITIONAL SAILOR'S PASTIME CHILDREN WHO WEAR ORTHODONTIC BRACES SHOULD REPORT TO THE RECREATION DECK AT 10.00 HRS. UGLIEST BRACE WINS A PARASCENDING EXPERIENCE OF A LIFETIME. YOU WILL BE HOISTED UP THE MAIN MAST BY A ROPE ATTACHED TO THE FRONT OF YOUR BRACE AND FLOWN FROM THE CROW'S NEST LIKE A PENNANT. SEE HOW GOOD YOUR DENTIST IS. HOW LONG WILL THE BRACE HOLD BEFORE IT SNAPS AND SENDS YOU PLUNGING INTO THE DEPTHS? MUCH MIRTH FOR ALL INVOLVED (EXCEPT FOR YOU, OBVIOUSLY).

FOLDING AND IRONING THE JOLLY ROGER 14.00 HRS IN THE LAUNDRY. ANYONE JOLLY CALLED ROGER HAD BETTER RUN AND HIDE.

TIMBER SHIVERING 17.00 HRS NAUGHTY CHILDREN ARE TIED TO THE BOTTOM OF THE BOAT WHILE TRAINED DOLPHINS PACK THEM IN ICE! ONE FOR THE CAMERA.

DINNER

THE FOLLOWING GUESTS ARE INVITED TO TAKE ~~POISON~~ SUPPER AT THE CAPTAIN'S TABLE. CHARLIE CHICKEN, ELIZA TOADLEY, HUMPTY EGG, EUSTACE COLON, PETAL STALEWATER, BART THUMPER.

WEATHER REPORT

WET, WET, WET! AFTER A WEEK ON BOARD MY SHIP YOU'LL BE A WRECK TOO!

CAPTAIN NIGHT-NIGHT PORTER

Avast, me hearties! I've developed a new accent since I moved into the SS *Pain and Everlasting Torment* down here on the bottom of the ocean — ha ha. so I have. Jim lad! I've developed a few more tentacles and all. Got them coming out my ears now.

Don't go. If you say you'll be mine I'll upgrade you to the Mermaid Suite. It's got a special bed made from a giant clam which closes when you're asleep to keep you nice and snug inside its stomach.

Yes. It's a bit wetter down here than what most people expect. Thought you'd be getting a nice dry room in the Hothell Darkness. didn't you? Full up. I'm afraid. Too many wicked children in the world needing to be taught a lesson. So I'm bringing the ~~overkill~~ (oops!) overspill down here to this ~~prison~~ (what is wrong with my fins? I can't seem to hold on to this pen!) cruise ship. Shame it's sunk. though. Makes sunbathing on the sun deck a bit tricky. And the swimming pool's not easy to use neither. Swimmers with water-wings keep floating out into the Gulf Stream. Last week there was a big scare when we thought a girl called Sylvia was drowning. Turned out she was only waving! Bit of a show-off. Sylvia. So I showed her off to a tiger shark and she was still waving when both her legs disappeared.

Of course YOU should be down here. This is a place where bad people come and you're obviously a bad 'un. because you're showing all the tell-tale signs — little fingers. squeaky voice. less than five feet tall. cry a lot. I bet you like sweets too. Thought so.

Answer these questions without thinking about the answers:

1. When you look at the weird behaviour of your parents and other adults do you sometimes feel that you must have come from a different planet?

2. Have you ever worn your pants outside your trousers?

3. When you go into a phone box do you have a strange urge to rip your clothes off?

4. Do you wish you could see through walls?

If you have answered yes to these questions you THINK you are a Superhero. but trust me. you're not. If you think you are better than all the rest. think again. It is impossible for children to be Superheroes because they are too wicked. They are all SuperZeroes. worthless wastes of skins who deserve everything this ship can throw at them. To prove it I have a test I perform on all my guests (of which lucky old you will shortly be one!) I call it my INFALLIBLE OIL DRUM TEST. I tie a one ton oil drum to your ankle then send you off for a swim. If you float you are a Superhero. If you sink to the sea bed you are clearly weighed down by your wickedness which makes you a Class 'A' SuperZero! It never fails.

I'm not scared of anything!

I'm the best musical statuer in the world!

I'm the cleverest everest!

I'M A WORM'S WORST NIGHTMARE!

**I'M THE MOST LOVED LITTLE GIRL
IN THE UNIVERSE!**

I'M THE HOTTEST BOTTOM IN THE WEST!

Those are the noisy children in the SuperZero corridor. Full of themselves that lot. Need bringing down a peg or two. I should explain. I've got all six of them hanging on coat hooks over a pit full of leopard sea snakes. A couple of pegs lower and the snakes should just about be able to reach the kiddies' toes!

I'm not scared of anything!

Ooh. I do like a challenge! And there's none quite as challenged as Charlie Chicken.

CAPTAIN NIGHT-NIGHT PORTER

FATAL ATTRACTION

'Your honour, the question we should be asking is this: why did the chicken cross the road?'

'Are you making fun of my court, Mr Hackle?'

'No, your honour. This extraordinary case begs an answer to that question. The case of that wicked boy you see incarcerated over there inside that anti-magnetic goldfish bowl to stop him snatching our watches and jewellery. If today we can find the answer to why the chicken crossed the road, you will have discovered the truth about this case and justice will have prevailed.'

'And what is your opinion, Mr Hackle, as Counsel for the Prosecution?'

'That the accused did deliberately and most foully cross the road without any consideration for the traffic thereon.'

'And Mr Fluff, for the defence, what say you?'

'Your honour, my client, Master Charlie Chicken, claims temporary insanity brought on by a traumatic surgical procedure as a child …'

'He still *is* a child!'

'As a *younger* child, your honour. He would no more run out in front of the traffic than plunge his head into the gaping jaws of a fox.'

'Is that meant to be a joke?'

'No, your honour, forgive me. I was forgetting that your name was Fox.'

'Well, don't let it happen again or I'll come round to your house tonight and rummage through your dustbins. Would somebody care to start me off … preferably at the beginning?'

* * *

The beginning was simple. Charlie Chicken lived in a family of girls. No father, just four elder sisters: Cheryl, Charlotte, Chipolata and Chips. When the girls and their mother started talking, the house fairly buzzed with cluck. In order to be heard above the clamour, Charlie had learnt to do three things. The first was to shout …

'CAN WE START SUPPER NOW, IT'S MIDNIGHT!' Here, the loudness of his voice was the key. The second was to lie …

'Brad Pitt wants me as his body double.' Here, the outrageousness of his comment was what grabbed their attention and left them panting to know more.

The third was to do dangerous things: jump out of the loft, juggle with knives and forks, climb between windows on the *outside* of the house. If there was one thing guaranteed to raise a scream or five it was danger!

Or sea slugs in pyjamas.

* * *

The judge groaned. 'Tell me we're not going to hear his *whole* life story!'

'No, your honour. I was merely trying to establish that what he did was as a result of his upbringing.'

'Everyone always tries to blame the parents, Mr Fluff. Did Mrs Chicken encourage Charlie to do these dangerous things?'

'Quite the opposite, your honour. She tried to stop him.'

'Exactly. I prefer to blame the culprit and punish him accordingly! Now let's get cracking!'

* * *

While Charlie kept the three of these attention-seeking tricks-in-the-home his life remained on an even keel, but when he started lying at school his life span off the road and crashed into a forest of concrete trees.

I've got a special cabin down here for little liars called the Banter Claws Suite. If they can talk themselves out of sharing a bed with six thousand deaf lobsters they deserve their freedom.

The original lie was told five minutes into a Monday Maths class, when Charlie suddenly decided that this was the day he would become a Superhero.

'Er, excuse me, Miss,' he said. 'Could I have a private word?'

'No!' replied his teacher, Miss Wattle. 'If it's worth saying you can say it in front of the whole class.'

'But it's top secret,' persisted Charlie. 'If what I'm about to tell you leaks out and I don't know where the leak came from I'll have to kill everyone in this room.'

'Would you like a detention?' asked Miss Wattle.

'Very well,' said Charlie. 'Miss Wattle … Class … I think you should know that the world is under threat from a flaming meteor and I am the only person who can save the planet. I haven't told you before because I have to keep my identity secret, but I am a Superhero.'

'Take *four* detentions,' she said.

'You must do what you must do, Miss Wattle, but so must I! I'm sorry, but I have to leave this lesson now to fly into the stratosphere and deflect the meteor off course with my special meteor-deflecting jumper!'

'Would this have anything to do with the test I'm just about to give you?' asked the teacher.

'Not at all,' protested Charlie. 'I love your tests, but if it's a choice between doing your test and letting the earth die, I think I know where my duty lies.' And he got up and left.

* * *

Of course, his lie had *everything* to do with missing the test, but none of the children realised this because, being children, they had fallen in love with the notion that they were at school with a Superhero. At break they begged Charlie to tell them it was true.

'Of course,' he said, continuing the fiction and receiving an awe-filled 'Ooooh!' for his trouble.

'And *did* you save the planet?'

'Well, it's still here, isn't it?' he said casually.

'So as a Superhero do you do dangerous things?' asked an easily impressed boy called Fidelius Minor. He was an elastic-boned child with floppy limbs and flesh as a soft as a jellyfish. The closest Fidelius Minor had ever come to danger was eating a slice of ham two days after its sell-by date.

'Of course I do dangerous things,' boasted Charlie. 'In the course of my job I have so far had to walk on glass, eat fire, and stop a stampede of buffalo with a high-powered jet of superpee.'

'So what's your Superhero name?' asked Fidelius Minor. There was a miniature pause while Charlie pretended to take a fly out of his eye, when in fact he was doing a bit of quick-thinking.

'FastMan!' he declared with a swagger.

'That's a bit boring,' murmured the crowd.

'I mean StrongMan,' he said quickly to stop everyone from leaving.

'Does that mean you work in a circus?' asked Madison, a sceptical girl in spherical spectacles.

'I mean FearlessMan!' shouted Charlie. 'Because I know no fear!'

'That's more like it,' cheered Fidelius Minor.

'Now I believe you!' So FearlessMan it was!

* * *

Unfortunately for Charlie, this now meant that he had to live up to his lie. Every morning, his excited schoolfriends wanted to know what FearlessMan had been up to the night before.

'Heroic things,' he said. 'Basically, it started with me flying through a burning building to save a burning budgerigar, which I had to put out by diving into the Thames, where I bumped into a stranded Minky Whale, which I piggy-backed out to sea. But as it rolled over to wave goodbye it head-butted an oil tanker, which split down the middle and spilled its oil, which I had to drink to save the environment. Tasted foul and turned my tongue black, but that was the least of my problems, because while I was drinking it I swallowed a shark and required immediate surgery to have him removed from my stomach. Luckily, the captain of the next boat that came along was a pirate called Dr Blood so he knew what to do and he cut me open with his hook from the top of here to the bottom of here and whipped the shark out …'

Madison, the girl in spherical spectacles, was still

sceptical. 'Show us the scar then,' she said.

'Interesting you should ask that,' said Charlie, 'but I don't scar. I've got Superhero skin.'

'So if I was to prod you with this sharp stick you wouldn't bleed?' she said, sliding a kebab skewer out of her school bag.

'Not quite,' he laughed. 'When I'm wearing my FearlessMan suit nothing can pierce my skin. In my school clothes I'm as vulnerable as the next man.'

'*A suit!*' gasped gullible Fidelius Minor. 'Did you hear that, everyone? FearlessMan has got a suit! Tell us what colour it is, FearlessMan.'

'I bet it's brown,' interrupted Madison, 'so that when he gets scared and has a bottom-malfunction it doesn't spoil the show.'

Brown's my favourite colour — after bloody stump red and mushy brain green.

Strangers like Madison did not have the patience of a mother or sister to indulge Charlie's fantasies. It was only a matter of time before FearlessMan had to stop *talking* about being fearless and *prove* it. So it was that one day Charlie Chicken asked his friends to tea and laid on a demonstration of his fearless

Superheroic powers in the garden. First up it was flying.

'And now, before your very eyes … behold! A boy can fly!'

The crowd snapped away on their mobile phones as he sprinted towards the garden wall, took off like a leaping salmon and landed feet first on top of the wall.

'Bravo!' shouted Fidelius Minor, bursting into fevered applause. Charlie took a bow and sneaked a sideways look at the trampoline (which he'd placed out of sight behind the Magnolia bush) to check it hadn't moved.

'What else can you do?' asked Madison.

'I can jump down again and miraculously fly over this magnolia bush,' said Charlie, leaping back down to earth then bouncing over the bush. Unfortunately, he lost control of his legs in mid-air, landed in a heap and Madison remained unimpressed.

'Right,' said Charlie, defiantly, 'you want to see fearless, then fearless it is!'

He marched his friends to another house and rang on the doorbell.

'Hello,' he said when the woman opened the door. 'I don't know you, do I?'

'No,' said the woman. 'I've never seen you before in my life.'

'And do you have a dog?'

'I do,' she said, in that wooden way that *bad* actors deliver lines. 'But don't let it lick your face or it might rip your nose off.'

'That's OK,' said Charlie Chicken, checking that his school friends were getting every word of this exchange. 'I am completely fearless so would love to kiss your dog's face while he is eating his dinner.'

'That *is* fearless!' cried Fidelius Minor. 'It incredibly stupid to kiss a strange dog's face while he's chewing chump chops!'

'OK,' said the woman. 'Why don't you and your friends come in while I find Fang.'

What Charlie *didn't* tell them was that the dog was not a stranger. It was twenty-one years old, didn't have any teeth and belonged to his auntie, who had been reading from a script that Charlie had written for her. It took Madison all of thirty seconds to work this out when she read the dog's collar tag.

My name is Old Smelly.
I am twenty-one years old and belong to
Charlie's aunt. I have no teeth so please
don't feed me solids. Just milkshakes.

Still determined to prove that his lies were real,
Charlie whisked his audience to the zoo
and put his arm inside the tiger's
cage.

'Now who else would do that, but
FearlessMan!' he declared, waving at
the tiger until it was so incensed that it
bit his hand off. Children screamed, watching-
mothers fainted, but Charlie did not even break
sweat. 'See how fearless and indestructible I am!' he
crowed at Madison. 'Now, if you'll excuse me, I
need to go somewhere private to grow a new hand.'
Then he walked round the back of the Safari Cafe
and chucked the remains of his false arm into a
wheelie bin.

Although the false-arm-in-the-tiger's-mouth
trick fooled a lot of people it did not fool
Madison, who noticed that the tiger had
spat out Charlie's arm. Clearly
polystyrene was not to its taste.

'How much more fearless do you want

me to be?' whispered Charlie after Madison had told everyone what she'd seen.

'More,' she said matter of factly. So 'more' it was, *much* more. *Everything* in fact.

* * *

Charlie Chicken's had one last trick up his sleeve. It was something so dangerous that it would prove his lie beyond all measure of doubt, and silence Madison for ever. When he announced his plan, Fidelius Minor fell to his knees and begged him to reconsider.

'Sorry,' said Charlie. 'My mind's made up.'

'Don't worry,' said the girl in the spherical spectacles. 'He won't do it. Chicken by name and chicken by nature.'

'We'll see.' Charlie smiled. 'Today, after school, in order to prove that I am not lying and really am FearlessMan I shall walk out into the traffic … blindfold!!!'

Of course, like all his other acts of fearlessness, this was another con. The stretch of road he'd chosen for his Walk of Death was next to a Pelican crossing, so he'd hear the beeps that accompanied the flashing green man and know when cars had come to a halt.

> LUCKILY, even the best-laid schemes of chickens often go awry!

* * *

After school, Charlie stood on the pavement while his school friends watched from behind the safety of the playground fence. Fidelius Minor was peeking through the gaps between his fingers as Charlie tied a scarf around his head. Then he turned to face the road, held his arms out in front of him and waited for the beeps.

And waited ...

And waited ...

Suddenly, he heard them. Without hesitating he pushed back his shoulders, stiffened his neck and stepped off the kerb. He did not expect what happened next. The first car screeched as it swerved past him, the second clipped his arm and the third picked him up and dashed him down like a ton of bull making mincemeat from a matador.

* * *

'Is that *it*!' roared the judge. 'Have I been sitting here all this time for *that*!' His eyes bulged from their sockets like two fat ladies diving for pearls. 'An idiotic boy who chooses to walk out into traffic without looking first deserves everything he gets!'

'It was bad luck,' explained Mr Fluff. 'The beeps he heard came from a reversing lorry not the pelican crossing!'

'Liars make their own luck,' growled the man in the wig. 'And I'm still waiting to hear why the chicken crossed the road!'

'Five minutes, your honour, and I'll explain.'

* * *

Charlie Chicken was scraped off the road and rushed to the hospital where he was poured out the back of the ambulance onto a trolley. A tearful Mrs Chicken paced up and down in the corridor outside his room while doctors came and went with X-rays and solemn faces. Then a female doctor sat Mrs Chicken down.

'There's nothing further we can do for him,' she said gently. 'Here's the number of an undertaker.' She leaned across and pressed a business card into Mrs Chicken's hand.

'Be sure to go and see them,' she said. 'And be sure to go round *the back*.' This seemed an odd thing to say, until Mrs Chicken looked at the card. On the front it read . . .

CYRIL SMITH UNDERTAKERS

But on the back was a handwritten note.

I shouldn't be giving you this, because he's not a proper doctor and I could lose my job. But take your son to see Dr Unethicus at the ChildSwap Hospital for Advanced BIONICS (Bad Infants Operated into Nice Infants Clinic). He's a strange, glassy-eyed quack, but he might be able to help. There's no time to waste. Good luck!

The ChildSwap Hospital for Advanced BIONICS was a dusty garage in the Ballspond Road. Dr Unethicus sat behind a desk which doubled as operating table and mortuary slab, winking with his one good eye.

'Puh!' he said, dismissing Charlie's injuries with a flick of his hand. 'I've stapled children back together again who were in much worse states than this. No, the real challenge of Advanced BIONIC surgery is to repair children for the better. Interested?'

'In what?' said Mrs Chicken.

'All it takes is a small slip of the scalpel …' Dr Unethicus smiled. 'It's a specialised service I recommend to all parents. You'd be amazed how many of them take me up on it.'

'Yes, but what are you offering to do?' she asked.

'While the boy is under I cut out the bits you don't like.'

'It's tempting,' said Mrs Chicken, 'but I'd prefer it if you could put something *in* instead – a double dose of fear to stop him doing dangerous things.'

'Impossible,' said the doctor, pushing his front tooth back into place with his tongue. 'Fingers, noses, hearts and minds, all of these I can alter, but emotions are strictly off limits.'

Which was a shame, because the injection of a little bit of fear into Charlie's brain would have gone a long way to undoing the damage that Dr Unethicus then went on to inflict.

* * *

Charlie woke up to hear the surgeon explaining the life-saving operation to his mother …

'The car made a right old mess, Mrs Chicken. Apart from the cuts and bruises his entire neural system was in tatters. His nerves had literally been torn to shreds. I've stripped them all out and replaced them with high-density steel wires which run from the tips of his toes to the top of his head where I've poked the ends into the back of his brain. So everything *should* work as normal.'

I'M A WORM'S WORST NIGHTMARE!

But when Charlie tried out his new body, he found that one vital ingredient was missing. He could see, hear, talk, smell and speak, but, because his nerves were now made of steel and steel does not transmit pain, he couldn't *feel* a thing. For the first time in his life, Charlie could honestly say that he knew no fear.

* * *

He challenged Madison in the playground on his first day back at school.

'Still think I'm *not* FearlessMan?' he scoffed, pressing his nose into her face. 'Then watch!' And he picked up a stag beetle from under the bike shed and clamped its pincers onto his finger. 'See?' he said unflinchingly. 'Nothing.'

'It's just another cheap trick,' she said, turning her back and walking away. For the rest of the day Charlie demonstrated his fearlessness to her at every opportunity by doing painful things and not reacting: sharpening his little finger in a pencil sharpener, nailing his ear lobe to his desk, sticking a compass through his nipple. By home time, he had convinced everybody *except* Madison that he had nerves of steel.

'A leopard does not change its spots,' she said.

'OK then,' he challenged. 'Tell me what *would* convince you that I was fearless.'

'Hmmm, let me see …' She laughed. 'Going back to the zoo, knowing what that tiger can do to a false arm, and giving him *your* real arm to eat.'

'And then you'd believe that I was a Superhero?'

'Either that or insane.'

'OK,' said Charlie. 'It's a deal.' He set off down the pavement at a lick and refused to stop, even when Madison cried,

'No! Stop! Wait! I didn't mean it. Charlie come back. I was joking!'

* * *

Mrs Chicken heard about the

accident at work. Her son had been stopped on the bus carrying a severed arm in a plastic bag. When asked what he was doing with it, he told the policeman that it was his and he was going to the hospital to have it sewn back on.

'But isn't it painful?' gasped the constable.

'Not at all,' said the one-armed boy, 'just a bit cold.'

Mrs Chicken was there at the bus stop when Charlie alighted. She grabbed the bag full of arm, wrapped the stump in her jumper, bundled him into a waiting taxi and whisked him off to the Ballspond Road.

I'm the best musical statuer in the world!

'Why've you come back to *me*?' asked Dr Unethicus, as Charlie lay sleeping on the table. 'They could have sewn his arm back on at the main hospital.'

'Because only you can help him,' she cried. 'Now that he can't feel pain, he won't stop doing dangerous things. He's going to kill himself. You have to remove his nerves of steel.'

The doctor dipped his staple gun into a basin of

whisky to sterilise it. 'Can't be done,' he said, firing the first shot into Charlie's arm. 'If I take out the steel now his body will collapse like a hollow blancmange.'

'So what can I do?' howled Mrs Chicken.

'I do believe there's only one option,' said the doctor. 'Look, his fingers are moving again.'

* * *

The judge wiped his brow with the hem of his robe. 'Are you sure you're not making this up, Mr Fluff?'

'No, your honour. Dr Unethicus magnetised Charlie Chicken's nerves of steel so that his mother could stick him to the fridge door and keep a constant eye on him. Only when he left the clinic in the Ballspond Road, he had travelled no more than ten yards before three dustbins, a hubcap and a small motorbike had attached themselves to his legs. Imagine what a shock it was! Charlie had no idea that this was going to happen. So when he passed the jewellers' less than a minute later and all of the gold and silver jewellery flew through the plate-glass window and jumped into his pocket, he was not to blame.'

'And that's your defence?' said the judge.

'Yes,' said Mr Fluff. 'Accidental jewel theft due to magnetic nerves of steel.'

'I see. And just out of interest, why did the chicken cross the road?'

'Well, initially, your honour, to prove that he was a Superhero. But more recently because of a magnetic attraction to a lamppost.'

'Which is how we caught him?'

'Yes, your honour. Stuck fast.'

The judge sucked in his cheeks and scratched his wig. 'Stand up,' he said to Charlie. They boy rose inside his anti-magnetic goldfish bowl. 'I don't believe a word of this,' he said. 'Magnetic nerves of steel! You're a self-confessed liar, so what else can I think except that you've robbed a jewellery store, got yourself caught and have cooked up this cock-and-bull story to get yourself off?'

'But it's true,' said Charlie.

'And the moon is made of cheese!' snorted Judge Fox. 'You're going down, Charlie Chicken, for a very long time!'

For ever in fact. Down, down, down to 40,000 leagues under the seal

The judge was so angry at Charlie for wasting his

time that he sentenced him to ten years in gaol, but when Charlie arrived in his cell block they couldn't prise him off the bars. A second judge ruled that Charlie probably *was* magnetic after all and, to save him causing any further damage, changed his sentence to ten years isolation in the middle of the Atlantic Ocean where there was no metal to mess up the punishment.

With no nails allowed, a sturdy raft was lashed together using tree trunks and twine. It was secured to the seabed with non-metallic rope and Charlie was rowed out to it in a wooden boat. The warders gave Charlie a sun hat, a supply of fresh water and a plastic fishing rod to catch food. Then the boat disappeared leaving Charlie on his own for the first time in his life.

The silence was unbearable. How he longed for the noisy cluck of his sisters and mother and the creak of a tall ship in which to sail home.

That night, as the moon burnt brightly in the star-speckled sky, Charlie heard a groan from underneath him like the cry of an angry water god. He thought it was a hurricane or an earthquake on the ocean bed, but it was neither of these things. Lumps of twisted black metal, fuzzy with water and age, burst out of the sea like scarred leviathans. Silhouetted against the moon these angry beasts crashed back into the water and sped across its surface towards the wooden raft where Charlie sat spellbound. All of the wrecks of all the boats and planes from all of the world wars throughout time had been sucked from their watery graves by his magnetic pull. And as you can imagine, with that much hardware on board, Charlie Chicken didn't stand a chance. The raft sank without trace and was never seen again.

So, in a strange way, Charlie *did* become a Superhero. What name shall we give him — MagnetMan or SuperWreck? You decide. And while you're deciding, work out if this story's true or not, and if you think not, how come Charlie's down here with me now? With all that hardware attached he's too big to fit in a cabin, so I've stuck him outside on the Promenade Deck like a great big metal sculpture, where he's very popular with the goldfish who swim in and out of his holes.

SUPERHEROES I WOULD LIKE TO SEE
No 643 – TearAChild'sTongueOutMan
It would make the world a whole lot quieter,
wouldn't it?

33

Now. I need you to imagine that you are an ordinary adult. You know, flabby belly, quick temper, and bags under the eyes from looking after short people like you. You've got a little daughter. it's her birthday party and you've organised a game of musical statues. You are standing at one end of the room holding a tape recorder while the children are dancing behind you waiting for you to stop the music, turn round and catch whoever's moving. Imagine that you have played this game ten times and each time the same girl has won. Let us call her Eliza, because that's her stupid name. Each time you switch off the music and turn round Eliza is the one who is standing rock still, while all around her the other children are wobbling and toppling to the floor. Naturally enough, you think she is the best at the game and smile encouragingly at her, and she does nothing to make you think differently. Indeed, she smiles back and melts your heart with her sparkling blue eyes, because she looks every inch the perfect child; as polite and pretty as pumpernickel pie!

Now imagine you had eyes in the back of your head. What do you think you would see while the music was on? Eliza playing fair and NOT pushing other girls and boys out of the way while your back is turned, or a monster who WAS? Time to find out . . .

LITTLE ANGEL

Eliza was the eldest child in the Toadley family. Below her there were two punch bags: her little brother Wycombe and the dog Buster or, as the neighbours thought, 'Bad Boy' (because that was all they ever heard him being called over the garden fence). Wycombe and Buster's lives ran along similar paths. Buster spent most of his life in the dog house, which was a chain attached to a sycamore tree at the bottom of the garden, while Wycombe spent most of his life in the bedroom, for having 'naughty bones' as his mother liked to say. Over and above being prisoners, what bound boy and dog together was the fact that neither had ever done anything wrong. They were always framed by another and that other was …

Come on! It doesn't take a genius to work it out. After all she is a BIG SISTER. and big sisters are second only in viciousness in the whole history of the planet to velociraptors.

35

… Eliza. She was *always* to blame and *always* clever enough NOT to get caught.

What was even more extraordinary about this family was that Eliza and Wycombe's parents, Mr and Mrs Toadley, were both police officers. Terry Toadley was a Detective who solved murder cases, while Laura Toadley cut up dead bodies looking for evidence that Mr Toadley could use to catch the killer. For example, if Terry thought that a person had been beaten to death by a large pelican, he would ask his wife to look for evidence of fish in the victim's stomach, the discovery of which would prove conclusively that the victim had been eating out of the pelican's bucket of fish when the pelican had tiptoed up from behind and done him in with its beak. The point is, that of all the parents in the world not to notice that the innocent child was getting the blame while the guilty one was getting away scot-free, Detective Constable Terry Toadley and Forensic Detective Laura Toadley were the last ones you'd think of.

***

It all started at Stacey Beanbag's birthday party when Eliza was nine. It was the first time she had ever played musical statues and she took to it like a

Chinese torturer to water. While the judge had her back turned and the music was playing Eliza bit, punched, tripped and shoved her fellow competitors in the back so that when the music stopped and the judge looked round, Eliza was the only player standing perfectly still with her perfect smile and perfectly twinkling blue eyes.

As she was leaving Stacey's house (not a moment too soon for Stacey), Eliza spotted an old copy of the celebrity magazine *HOT!* on the hall table. It had an article inside about the mysterious disappearance of the World Champion Musical Statuer, Sneak Ferret, who'd famously beaten up his little sister then vanished after winning the title last year. Eliza slipped the magazine under her coat and read it on the way home.

***

Ten minutes later, when she burst through the front door, she was full of her new idea.

'I want to be the new World Champion Musical Statuer!' she cried.

'Since when?' asked her father.

'Since I just played musical statues and realised I was brilliant,' she said modestly. 'Since I just read this magazine and imagined *my* face of the front cover!

Just think of it, daddy, your little angel as famous as Paris Hipbone and Christine Anaconda!'

'My little angel, my little star,' gushed her proud, but delusional father, wiping tears of hope from his eyes.

Now that she had her sights set on becoming the best musical statuer in the world Eliza had to practise three skills: standing still, smiling sweetly and cheating. She had worked out that the winner of musical statues was invariably the person who could knock the other players off-balance without getting caught by the judge. The more she practised the nastier she became.

Down here. nasty children make excellent shark bait or. if you knot their feet behind their neck. a playful bouncy ball for a baby squid.

She smashed china ornaments and blamed it on Buster's tail, she ripped newspapers and blamed it on his teeth, she broke wind and blamed it on his bottom. And when the white sofa was covered in mud, even though it was she who'd been outside in the garden burying a dead budgerigar, she fingered Buster as the culprit.

'It *must* be Buster,' she said with wide-eyed innocence.

'Then how come Buster's paws are clean while your hands are dripping with mud?' asked her mother.

'I don't know,' she said calmly. 'It wasn't me.'

'Oh, now I don't know anymore,' angsted  her mother, who was brilliant at extracting the truth from a tiny hair underneath a corpse's fingernail, but couldn't see it when it was staring her in the face wearing bright pink knickers and a glitter wig. 'I was sure it was you, Eliza, because of the mud on your hands, but you *never* lie so if you say it wasn't you, then it wasn't.'

'HELLO!' shouted Wycombe. 'She's pulling the wool over your eyes. She's got muddy hands because she did it!'

'I've got muddy hands because I have just used them to wipe the mud off Buster's paws,' she said. 'Satisfied?'

Buster knew then that the game was up and took himself off to the Dog House, while the fool, Mrs Toadley, burst into tears.

'I'm such a bad mother for suspecting it was you in the first place,' she wailed.

'Yes you *are*,' confirmed Eliza, 'but after today, maybe you'll have learned your lesson.' Then she left the room and deliberately bumped into Wycombe so that she could give him a dead leg. 'As for you,' she hissed in his ear, 'you're going straight to Hell!'

Anything that couldn't be blamed on the dog was blamed on Wycombe. The list was unending: breaking mum's hairbrush, flooding the bathroom, laddering mum's tights ...

'But I don't wear tights,' protested Wycombe when his mother confronted him with the evidence.

'Your sister says you wore them to rob a bank,' she said. 'And anything our little angel says must be true!'

... burnt pans, lost keys, phone messages that were never passed on ...

'Somebody forgot to tell me that granny died and now we've missed the funeral!' shouted Mr Toadley. 'My own mother dead and I never said goodbye!' Without letting anyone see, Eliza slid the yellow post-it-note out of her pocket – Tuesday 4.30 – GRANDPA PHONED. GRANNY DEAD. PLEASE CALL BACK – pressed it into Wycombe's hand and shouted, 'Oh what is that in your hand, Wycombe?'

'That's not fair,' he cried. 'I've never seen it before in my life.'

'Bad boy!' growled his sister. 'Go to your bedroom.'

'I'm not a dog,' he said.

… piles of dirty clothes in the bathroom, huge telephone bills, and hair dye in the kitchen sink.

'Am I the one with wet hair?' protested Wycombe. He pointed to his sister who was standing next to the sink with dripping wet hair and a towel round her shoulders. 'No. That's Eliza. And what is the colour of the hair dye all over the walls and work-surfaces? It is red. I have got black hair. Eliza has got red *dyed* hair. Even a detective should be able to work that one out.'

'But I didn't do it.' Eliza smiled. 'I may have been washing my hair, but I wasn't using hair dye. That was Wycombe. He was pretending it was blood. It was him who squirted it over the eggs and plates and white linen tea towels.'

'Wycombe …' snarled Mr Toadley.

'It wasn't me,' protested the boy.

'Then why are you holding the bottle of red hair dye in your hand?' asked his smug sister.

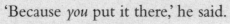

'Because *you* put it there,' he said.

'And why would I do that?'

'Because you heard mum and dad coming through the front door, shoved it in my hand and wound an elastic band around my fingers so I couldn't get them open again!'

Eliza shook her head at disappointment speed. 'Does that sound likely?' she said. 'Does that honestly sound like the sort of thing your little angel would do?'

Her parents melted like chocolate peanuts in her hand. 'Not our little angel,' they said. Then they barked at the culprit. 'And *you* can go to your room!'

I'M A WORM'S WORST NIGHTMARE!

Not when you're dead, Eustace!

***

The Musical Statues World Championship was held in a gothic castle called Gargoylia slap bang in the middle of Dartmoor where wolves howl. As the Toadleys' car turned off the road and trekked up the drive towards the drawbridge that lay across the castle's moat, twisted black ribbons of bats swirled around the central tower that was held up by a dozen flying buttresses. Below the castellations and just above the top-floor windows, stretched like one long eyebrow across the castle's face, was a ledge which ran all the way around the roof. Perched along this ledge were the creatures that gave this castle its name: hunched devils with horns, tails and talons; fire-breathing monsters with lions' heads, goats' bodies and the tails of serpents; winged humanoids, laughing, leering and spitting on the heads of those below. These were stone gargoyles, protectors, defenders, and as Eliza was shortly to find out, spirits of eternal vengeance!

When the car stopped, Eliza was first out, dragging Wycombe behind her.

'I'm *this* close to winning this title and becoming famous,' she hissed in his ear. 'Get in my way and I will squash you like a worm. I don't want to see you anywhere near the competition tomorrow, because I'm here to win and you'll just distract me with your stupid face!'

'And what if I say no?' said Wycombe. 'What if I said I'll do it, but only if you're nice to me for a change and use the word *please*?'

Eliza's answer was swift and direct. With one

shove she propelled Wycombe off the bank and into the muddy water of the moat.

'Help!' he cried.

'Oh, Mummy, quick!' shouted Eliza. 'Wycombe's fallen in the water.'

'She pushed me!' Wycombe shouted in the darkness.

'Oh, Daddy,' she pleaded, 'I wasn't pushing him, I was trying to save him by grabbing hold of the back of his coat.'

'You little angel,' said her father.

'We were blessed the day we had you,' said her mother.

'I'm still in the water,' said her brother.

And Eliza just smiled. 'I am a little bit special, aren't I?' she said.

But the gargoyles didn't think so. Their cold, stone eyes were singularly unimpressed.

***

That night, while Mr and Mrs Toadley occupied the Sherlock Holmes Suite and Eliza luxuriated in her Princess four-poster bed, Wycombe tossed and turned on a straw mattress in the attic. He had caught a cold from swimming in the moat and Eliza had begged her parents not to let him sleep anywhere near her in case he passed on the germs and wrecked her chances of becoming world champion.

It was three o'clock in the morning and Wycombe was still awake. His room was just underneath the roof and an eerie wind whistled through the gaps between the tiles. Suddenly, he heard scratching at the window. It sounded like a stone being scraped across a plate. Through his threadbare curtains he could see the shadow of a hunched figure with pointed wings hanging from the ledge above his window. The scratching became more urgent.

'What do you want?' whispered Wycombe bravely.

'Let me in,' said the voice outside. It had a strange ring to it, like millstones grinding in an echo chamber. 'I need to tell you something.'

'No way,' stuttered the boy. 'If you're what I think you are you're staying outside.'

'Come closer,' cajoled the voice almost playfully. 'Draw the curtain. Discover.' Despite his misgivings Wycombe found himself climbing out of bed.

'I'm *not* scared,' he said as he lifted one corner of the curtain and peeked outside. A stone face with a puffy tongue and gruff green beard leered back. Wycombe fell backwards with shock, pulling the curtain and its pole off the wall.

'Shall I tell you why the musical statue competition is held in *this* castle every year?' asked the gargoyle at the window. 'It's for *you*.'

'For *me*?' said the startled boy.

'Well *this* year,' explained the statue. 'Last year it was for a poor girl called Cynthia Ferret.'

'The sister of Sneak Ferret?'

'And very happy she is now too!'

Like the detective he one day hoped to become, Wycombe was slowly piecing together the jigsaw. 'Would I be right in assuming,' he asked, 'that you know what happened to her brother?'

The gargoyle raised a stone eyebrow.

'He *didn't* disappear, did he?'

'No,' it rasped, pointing back up to the ledge with its wing tip. 'Third chimera on the left.'

'Gosh,' said the boy. 'Gosh!'

What a polite boy Wycombe is!

Wycombe was so intrigued by this gargoyle's story that he opened the window and let it in. They sat on the end of the bed and chatted like old friends.

'Children who are nasty to their brothers and sisters, but are clever enough not to be caught, are always good at musical statues. So we started the world championships at Gargoylia. Now every year the baddest children compete and my fellow gargoyles and I and come down from our ledge to right all wrongs. This year it's your sister's turn. She boasts she has a sixth sense to detect when something is creeping up behind her. Let's put that to the test, shall we?'

'You're not asking for my permission, are you?' said Wycombe.

'No,' said the gargoyle. 'The decision has been made.'

'So when's it going to happen?'

'When the music stops, of course.'

'Oh, right,' said the boy, not understanding what that meant. 'And *how* do you do it?'

'Trade secret,' it said. 'All I *can* say is this: it's positively petrifying.' And with that, he flapped his stone wings and was gone.

***

All the next day, Wycombe sat patiently outside the Grand Hall, where the competition was being held, listening to the music stopping and starting and receiving snippets of information about Eliza's progress from one or other of his parents.

'She's in the semi-final now.'

'It's between her and a horrible-looking boy called Claude Foot.'

'He cheats, you know. When the judge's back is turned he pushes other children over to gain an advantage.'

'Does Eliza not do that as well?' asked Wycombe.

'Good heavens, no!' exclaimed his mother. 'Eliza would never do anything so sneaky. She's our little angel!'

But Wycombe knew that she would and *was*. From what he could see through the keyhole, before turning on that sunny smile, she was pushing, stamping, punching and kicking with the best of them.

***

She won, of course. No more than she'd expected. She was gowned and crowned the Musical Statues Champion of the World. Press photographs were taken of her in various frozen poses, then the family was asked to join her on her throne for a group portrait. It was only then that Wycombe was allowed into the hall to sit at his sister's knee like a dog. She kicked him in the small of the back each time the photographer cried, 'Cheese!' so that when the shutter clicked he was always grimacing.

'They'll have to airbrush you out of all the photos now!' she whispered in his ear as she left the hall to disrobe. Before the winner's party she had to return her crown to the cabinet where it lived all year round. In the corridor outside the Grand Hall she saw an arrow pointing up some spiral stone steps to the Disrobing Room. There were over a hundred steps and she arrived out of breath at a wooden door which had a sign on the handle.

OPEN ME

How very strange, she thought, but the crown and cloak were heavy and she wanted to get rid of them. She pushed the door and entered an empty room.

'Hello,' she called, noticing that the window was wide open. As she walked across to look out, as the door slammed shut behind her and the key turned in the lock. She span round, hearing what she thought was a heavy stone being dragged across the floor, but nobody was there. Just a faint cloud of dust speckled with particles of green beard. 'Who's there?' That was when the music started. It seeped through the ceiling and walls. It filled up the room like poisoned gas. Chopin's *Death March* played on a thundering church organ. 'What's going on?' panicked the girl. 'Is this your idea of a game, Wycombe?'

'Not Wycombe, no!' sniggered a voice in her ear. Again she span. Again she could see nothing behind her.

'It's Claude Foot, isn't it? You're angry because I won and you didn't?'

Now the voice laughed, drawing so close to Eliza's back that the hairs stood up on her neck. She could feel puffs of cold, damp breath on her skin.

'Who are you?' Her voice was strangled with fear, yet slowly she turned.

The gargoyle's face was pressed up against hers. The red eyes blazed, the mouth roared and the slimy yellow tongue quivered like a corn snake. 'Welcome to the ugly club!' it howled, reaching out with its chiselled claws. 'You're one of us now!'

'Stay away from me,' she cried, her heart beating like a stonemason's hammer.

'Stay away ...' But she never finished her sentence. As the gargoyle touched her shoulder the words froze on her lips. Her skin turned grey and her flesh became stone. Her terror had literally petrified her.

Well, stone me!

Needless to say, when Eliza didn't turn up at the party, Mr and Mrs Toadley were distraught. They brought their detective skills into play and hunted high and low for their daughter, but they were city police-people and this was the countryside, and without cups of coffee and doughnuts to feed their brains they didn't know where to start. Three days after the competition they were no nearer to finding their little angel, so they gave up and went home without her.

In the car before they left, a sad Mr Toadley turned to Wycombe who now occupied the back seat alone. 'It's just the three of us now, Wycombe,' he said. 'Shall we bury the past, turn over a new leaf and agree to get along?'

'I'd like that,' said the boy. 'And I give you my word that from now on I'll never be naughty again.' Which wasn't a difficult promise to make, because he'd never been naughty in the first place.

***

Had they looked up towards the sky, of course, they would have seen their daughter staring down at them, sitting on the ledge with her screaming face and stone-cold wings (which came as standard with every gargoyle makeover). But they didn't, which was a shame, because for the first time in her life, Eliza actually *looked* like a little angel – albeit an ugly one with a gruff green beard made from lichen and moss.

Last month, I got the gargoyles to drop her off down here in the *Pain and Everlasting Torment*. They got an albatross to scoop her off the ramparts and carry her out to sea. When it dropped her into the water she sank like a stone. I've kept her busy, because on a ship there are hundreds of uses for a stone statue. She's been a doorstop, a figurehead, an Atlas Stone in the World's Strongest Pirate competition, a useless object for the little horrors to deface with acrylic paint in the Water Babies' Kindergarten, a pumice stone for an itchy Elephant Seal and an anchor. In fact ,she's down on the sea bed now, buried up to her neck in coral flakes!

I'm the cleverest everest!

That's Humpty Egg. Thinks he's a braniac, but he's not all he's cracked up to be!

Have you ever noticed how parents tend to be competitive with other parents where the intelligence of their offspring is concerned? It is rare, for example, to hear a father say of his son, 'Boy's a real loser. Takes after me. We thought we'd forget about school and send him straight to prison seeing as that's where he's going to be spending most of his adult life.' Or indeed a mother to say of her daughter, 'She's certainly not going to be a model with a great fat nose like

53

that, is she? Unless they want a model for pork sausages! Darling, make that noise you always make when you speak. You know, oink oink!' It is generally accepted that parents think their children are the most perfect human beings ever created.

Oh. that it were true . . .

THE FLAT-PACK KID

When Humpty Egg was born his parents doted on him. They marvelled at his little hands and feet, they clapped when he blew spit bubbles out of his mouth and they proudly took his nappy round to the neighbours to show them what he'd made out of supper. There was *nothing* about their baby that they did not find fascinating. So when Humpty Egg started to show an unusual interest in how the world worked, they actively encouraged his enquiring mind. They laughed gaily when he tore apart his rattle and threw it in the sink grinder, they cheered when he dismantled his cot and left it in bits on the floor, and they wept with joy when he unscrewed the back off an electric fire and dumped it in the bath. Far from telling him off for breaking things, they raved about his 'Egg-cellent mind' in newspaper articles and threw parties in his honour at which they would boast to friends, family and strangers about how clever Humpty was.

'He's only six months old and already he can strip down a Royal Enfield rifle,' they would say to a crowded room full of politely smiling people. 'He's probably the cleverest child of his generation.' And guests would nod their heads and say …

'Really?' Or …

'Fancy that.' Or if they were particularly creepy … 'Three cheers for the Egghead!'

> **I'M THE MOST LOVED LITTLE GIRL IN THE UNIVERSE!**

> That's what I love about SuperZeroes. They're so modest.

Eventually however, the day dawned when Humpty's vandalism stopped being funny. To Mr Egg, that is. In the beginning he didn't mind clearing up after his son, mending broken furniture, plastering walls and gluing the heads back onto ornaments, but as the months went on and the jobs got bigger and the spillage of his precious blood increased, he *did*. For all his enthusiasm, Mr Egg was not a good DIY-er. Chisels, saws and hammers seemed to love the taste of his fingers. So on this particular day, with blood gushing out of a hole in his thumb and the washing machine in bits on the floor, it was hardly surprising that Mr Egg threw his screwdriver through a window and bellowed,

'*Let somebody else tidy up after this horrible little boy!*'

Mrs Egg, who had still to recognise the evil in her son, covered dear Humpty's ears and called her husband, 'Cruel! That's what you are,' she said. 'You're a brute of a father, Alan. Our baby boy was only exercising his enquiring mind.'

While Humpty laughed at his mother's tears, Mr Egg stomped into the hall to call a handyman. On the telephone table there was a pile of unsolicited business cards. He picked up the one on top and dialled the number.

***

Not long after, there was a strange whirring noise outside the front door followed by the heaving bellows of a sigh. Mr Egg opened the door to see a strange bicycle drop out of the sky and land in their front garden. Welded to the crossbar was a helicopter rotor blade on a mast and behind the back wheel, attached to the frame by an aluminium bar, was a floating trailer held up by a tiny hot-air balloon. Sitting on the bike was a small man with a large yellowing moustache. He had comb-over hair and wore a pair of blue overalls which had the letters DIY DAVE printed on the back. He jumped off his bike, clicked open the lid of his trailer, took out a metal box brimming with power tools and walked towards the front door.

'Good morning,' he said in a boring monotone. 'DIY Dave at your service. Now, I know what you're thinking: what exactly is Dave's mode of transport? Let me fill you in, Mr Egg. This is my bicycle, helicopter, balloon transportational vehicle which I have cleverly called my Balloocyclopter. You can probably see what I've done there. I've put the three words together. Rather inspired. Took me about three weeks to think of that and only two weeks to build it! Now, where's the problem?'

When DIY Dave saw the mess that Humpty had made of the washing machine he shook his head and tutted so loudly that Mrs Egg leapt to her son's defence.

'I think it's important to encourage a child's enquiring mind,' she said. 'I mean, I know Humpty's not clever enough to go to university yet, but he really is very advanced for his age. In fact, I think he's probably one of the top three cleverest children in the world, if not *the* top. I mean, I don't want to go overboard about it, but he is super-clever, Nobel-prize winning material, if you ask me. In my opinion, to be able to dismantle a washing machine at nine-months-old is quite something!'

But instead of smiling indulgently at Humpty as everyone else did, DIY Dave spoke his mind. 'He can take stuff apart, Mrs Egg. That's all very well, but can he put it back together again? Now that *would* be clever.'

Humpty's mother squeaked with indignation. 'What do you expect, you stupid man, he's only nine-months-old!'

'So you said,' said DIY Dave. 'There we are. All done.' He didn't want to be paid for the work. 'If I never have to clear up after Humpty again,' he explained, 'that will be payment enough. Goodbye, Mrs Egg.'

Then he turned to her husband and fixed him with a meaningful stare. 'I do hope I won't be coming back,' he said, 'for Humpty's sake.' Then he picked up his power tools and went outside only to discover that somebody in nappies had taken the wheels off his Balloocyclopter.

***

Unfortunately, Humpty did not heed DIY Dave's warning. As he grew up he worked his way through his parents' precious possessions. He destroyed record players, boilers, garage doors, cat flaps, shower pumps, burglar alarms and at least six vacuum cleaners. Mindful that DIY Dave did not want to be called out again, Mr Egg tried to repair the damage himself, but he couldn't. He didn't have do-it-yourself hands. He had a break-it-yourself hand on the end of his right arm and a pick-up-the-phone-and-get-someone-else-to-do-it-for-you hand on the end of his left. So despite his warning, DIY Dave was called back time after time and on each occasion refused payment. Instead, he simply repeated his mantra, 'If I never have to clear up after Humpty again, that will be payment enough.' But Humpty *never* cleared up after himself.

Even a smelly old dog kicks leaves over it.

***

It was Humpty's eleventh birthday. To celebrate, he rose early and dismantled the central heating system. Mr and Mrs Egg woke to find icicles inside their bedroom window and a bath so cold that flies were doing backstroke in the water to keep warm. DIY Dave got the call and duly arrived with his box of power tools. Only on this occasion he wasn't smiling, and when Humpty tried to dismantle the handyman's new hammer-action drill his eyes flashed with anger.

'Never touch my tools,' he growled. 'They are my children, Master Egg. If it wasn't for my power tools I wouldn't be so powerful.'

'You're not powerful,' sneered Humpty. 'You're just a bodger on a bicycle.'

DIY Dave leant towards the boy and whispered in a sinister voice, 'You would do well to take me seriously for I am more powerful than a mayfly.'

Humpty's mother couldn't help herself. 'Mayflies aren't powerful,' she snorted. 'Mayflies only live for one day.'

'And with so little time to live they have no time to regret,' explained the handyman. 'In the insect kingdom, this makes them uniquely clear-headed. Their solutions are brutally efficient. No conscience, Mrs Egg, just like me!'

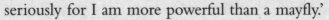

DIY Dave had said his piece. He brushed down his overalls and picked up his box of tools. 'Many happy returns of the day, master Humpty. Enjoy it to the full, for it may be your last.' Then he turned to Mr and Mrs Egg. 'Now that your son is eleven he is old enough to know better. Should I be called out again to clear up his mess, because you can't do it yourself, I shall be forced to do him for you.'

'Do *him*?' gasped Mrs Egg. 'Do *what* to him?'

'Oh come now!' DIY Dave smiled. 'What do you think the DIY in my name stands for?'

'Do-it-yourself?' guessed Mr Egg.

'Oh dear me no!' chuckled the handyman. 'Do

IN, Mr Egg. Do IN …' He stopped in the doorway. 'Today, for the last time, there is no charge. *Next* time, if there *is* a next time, I shall extract from you and Humpty the full price. No discounts. Good day.'

The next minute passed in silence while DIY Dave remounted his Balloocyclopter and took to the skies. Finally, Mrs Egg voiced what the other two were thinking.

'He's gone all creepy,' she said, 'I don't think I want him back in this house.'

But two days later DIY Dave *was* back …

***

It was Sunday morning. Humpty's enquiring mind had been up since four, examining a loose flap of wallpaper in his bedroom. Keen to find out what was underneath he had peeled it back to reveal a wall made entirely from grey plaster. But that was not enough for Humpty. He needed to know what was underneath *that*. Using a pen to dig a large hole through the plaster he discovered wooden struts. Now he needed to know what was behind those … And so the destruction went on, until, having sawn through the struts and knocked out ninety-three roof tiles to give himself some light, Humpty found himself standing in the attic.

'Interesting!' he said. 'So my room is made out of walls and one of these walls hides the attic and supports the roof and when the roof falls in I can see the sky, which must, therefore, be suspended by some clever mechanism of nature above the house!' By now his enquiring mind had gone into overdrive. He had to find out how the house was built down to the very last nail.

That'll be the one in Humpty's coffin!

***

Two minutes later, as the first blow from the sledgehammer pulverised the bricks in their bedroom wall, Mr and Mrs Egg woke with startled grey faces.

'Just checking to see if you've got an attic next to your bedroom too,' announced Humpty.

They didn't, of course. Just the outside world, and it was rather cold and breezy.

'Oh isn't that lovely,' cried Mrs Egg, sitting up in bed. 'Clever old Humpty's given us the view I've always wanted. Look! We can see the traffic now.'

'And they can see *us*!' roared a furious Mr Egg, as his wife waved back to a busload of pensioners.

'And what did you learn from bashing out another window, Humpty, dear?' she asked.

'That walls are nothing more than filled-in holes,' said Humpty who was tearing up the floorboards with a claw hammer. 'If I'm right, I bet there's another room under this one!'

'Oh! He has got an enquiring mind!' crowed Mrs Egg as a plank sprang up from the floor and hit Mr Egg across the cheek, embedding a rusty nail in his chin.

'Ow!' he yelped. 'Humpty, stop!'

'Will you stop shouting, Alan!' shouted Mrs Egg. 'The boy is only enquiring.'

'But we don't want DIY Dave coming back to do him in, do we?'

'Then don't phone him,' said Mrs Egg. 'Why do you always have to complicate things, Alan? He won't come round unless we call him, will he?'

***

Three hours later, however, even Mrs Egg had lost her cool. Humpty was digging in the cellar while she was trying to cook Sunday lunch.

'It's no good!' she wailed suddenly. 'The lunch is ruined. We've got no gas, no electricity and no water!'

Mr Egg exploded out of his chair and ran to the top of the cellar steps. 'Humpty!' he yelled. 'I thought I told you to stop.'

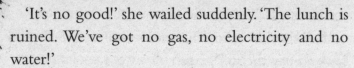

'Can't do that,' replied Humpty. 'I've still got loads of digging to do if I'm to find out whether the house is built on soil or not.'

'But you've dug through the amenities!'

'Can't hear you for the rushing water!' bellowed Humpty, making a sudden appearance on the cellar steps. He was soaked through to the skin. 'Maybe you're right,' he said. 'Maybe I should stop the digging till the water goes down a bit.'

At which point, an extraordinary thing occurred. The roof caved in, followed by the remaining walls, and the once-solid House of Egg crashed to the ground.

Of course, none of this would have happened if Humpty's mind had not been so enquiring.

When the dust settled, the Egg family were slightly startled to find DIY Dave sitting on the front lawn astride his Balloocyclopter.

'I *did* say,' he said, 'that next time I came you'd have to pay the full price.'

'Go away,' said Mrs Egg. 'We didn't call you. He's trespassing, Alan. Get rid of him!' But before Alan could move, DIY Dave danced across the grass with his cordless screwdriver and drove two six-inch screws through Mr Egg's feet.

'He's not going anywhere,' chuckled the creepy handyman, driving another two screws through Mrs Egg's slingbacks, 'and neither are you. Now then, Master Humpty—' the boy took a step backwards as DIY Dave picked up his box of power tools '—you were given fair warning and you ignored it. So now it is time to show you what a mayfly can do.'

Then, in a blur of arms and legs, he rushed Humpty. His power tools flashed like scimitars as they crunched through bone and screamed through sinew and ligaments. It was as if Humpty had been picked up by a ripping tornado full of grinding chainsaws and pump-action drills. His hands and feet poked fleetingly out of the squall of dust before being sucked back in. Then just as suddenly as DIY Dave had begun his punishment, it stopped. The handyman stepped out of the dust cloud and presented Mr and Mrs Egg with a bill.

CLIENT - HUMPTY EGG
CRIME - MAKING A MESS AND NEVER
TIDYING UP AFTER HIMSELF
COST - A FLAT-PACK KID

Then he pricked his finger with a chisel and used his own blood to write across the width of the piece of paper ...

PAID IN FULL

And with that, DIY Dave unscrewed Mr and Mrs Egg's feet and was gone.

The first thing they saw on the lawn was a cardboard box. Inside, Mr and Mrs Egg found their son, whose body had been neatly rearranged to pack down flat. DIY Dave had used a chainsaw to dismantle the boy into his component parts; arms, legs, hands, feet, fingers, toes, ears, nose, elbows, knees, neck and head. Then he had planed the boy's limbs until they were standard box size, drilled screw holes in his bones and placed him in the box ready for reassembly. But Mr and Mr Egg were no good at putting things back together again, and their feeble efforts were not helped by the assembly instructions being in a strange language that neither could understand, or by the fact that DIY Dave had forgotten to enclose any screws in the box.

That's *forgotten* as in the sense of *remembered, but thought it would be funny to leave them out*.

So they did what any sane parents would do. They phoned the Queen and asked her to send over some of her crack troops from the Royal IKEA Regiment to help them put Humpty together again, but the soldiers couldn't work out the instruction's either. After hours of trying, they gave up and put Humpty back in the box again.

***

By the time the soldiers had gone it was midnight and Mrs Egg was tired.

'Let's go to bed, Alan,' she said, 'and deal with Humpty's bits in the morning.'

She was forgetting, of course, that they didn't have a house, because Humpty had reduced it to rubble with his fiddling. So they slept in the garden shed and in the morning Mr Egg put on his dirtiest trousers and rebuilt the house himself. By the time it was finished, they had got used to sharing their life with a flat-pack kid and, to be quite honest, they preferred it. No more wrecked furniture; no more knocked-down walls and when they went on holiday they could send him on ahead by first-class post so they saved on the air fare.

And lying in his box in the hold of that aeroplane with all those hours to fill, Humpty had plenty of opportunity to flex that enquiring mind of his. With enquiries like,

'Why didn't I just put things back the way they were?' Oh well… better late than never!

I've put Humpty in the Games Room in a box marked JIGSAW. Nobody's managed to finish him yet. and a few pieces have unfortunately gone missing — one of his eyes. the front of his head. two fingers and his heart. Still. they're overrated hearts. Never saw the need for one. myself.

If I hear another word out of that anchor I'm going to melt her down into artificial fins and sell her to a Sturgeon (they're clever doctor fish who operate on other fish that are ill with fin rot)!

Here's a little poem what always makes me cry.*

ON THE HOOK
I am a little worm
Who's as happy as can be
There's only one place on the earth
That really worries me.
It's in the ocean's depths
Where the fishes swim so free
And chase me till I'm quite done in
And then devour me.

In the pantheon of Superheroes many take their form from nature: Batman. Catwoman. Spiderman. The Fly. Ordinary human beings utilize the strengths of animals, to increase their powers and enable them to fight crime. In the pantheon of SuperZeroes, however, the opposite is true. When bad human beings try to make themselves more powerful by drawing on the strengths of animals disaster *always* follows with pain, death and sometimes a trip to the vet but one short step behind. This is the tale of Eustace Colon; a real bad boy who was not a fish, but still bit off more than he could chew!

(* with laughter)

THE WORM

Eustace Colon ate worms, because Eustace Colon liked upsetting people. His parents tried to stop him, but he wouldn't listen.

'Eating worms will kill you,' said Mr Colon, as his son slapped the sixteenth wriggler inside his bun and took a bite.

'They can block up your belly and stop things passing through,' said his mother.

'I'll take a laxative,' cheeked Eustace.

'No you won't,' said his father. 'Because if you get a worm bomb stuck in the outflow pipe of your stomach you'll blow up like a balloon and explode!'

'You're human,' pleaded his mother. 'Leave the worms for the birds and fishes.'

'Maybe I *am* a bird or a fish,' Eustace sniggered, feigning fear to taunt his anxious parents. 'Oh! What is this fluttering under my T-shirt? Is it a pair of wings? No, look mummy, it's FINS!' His mouth fell

open when he laughed. His throat convulsed and he regurgitated the half-digested worms onto his bottom lip where they slapped around in a pool of pink froth.

'That's disgusting!' retched his mother.

'That's delicious!' roared Eustace.

His father grabbed him by his collar. 'Sometimes,' he said, his grey face taut with barely-controlled rage, 'I don't know what we did to deserve a son like you.'

Eustace smiled defiantly to hide his answer. Simple, he thought. You had my sister!

***

It was hardly his sister's fault. She hadn't asked to be born, but Eustace felt shoved to one side when she was. Standing on a chair outside the door to that special room in the hospital, peering through the round window at his parents bent over his sister's cot, he'd wanted to be in there with them, but strangers kept whisking him off to the café for a cherry slush puppy. And when Evie got home, the doorbell never stopped ringing with more people to see her. Grannies and grandpas, aunts and uncles, cousins and friends all swept past Eustace on the doormat and wiped their feet on top of his shoes.

That's why he hated Evie. That's why he started

eating worms – to stop people looking at *her* and make them look at *him* instead. But the first time Evie saw him eat a worm, her reaction was so fabulously loud and over the top that it gave Eustace a wicked idea. As she ran around the house screaming, 'Waaaaahhhuuuuurrrrrrrgggggh!' and buried herself in their mother's wardrobe, Eustace realised that he never needed to be jealous of her again, because he had the power to make her scream.

SUPERHEROES I WOULD LIKE TO SEE

No 1067 – FlannelBoy

No more tears at bathtime. Either dirty little children get clean without a fuss or FlannelBoy rinses them down the plughole!

From that day onwards Eustace became obsessed with worms and built himself a worm farm to supply his sister-teasing programme. If the family ate spaghetti for supper he would wait until Evie had cleaned her plate before saying casually, 'Oh dear I seem to have lost a load of my worms. I do hope they weren't hiding on your plate, Evie.'

'Waaaaahhhuuuuurrrrrrrgggggh!'

When she was sitting on the loo, he'd push worms through the keyhole and under the door. 'Quick, Evie! Save yourself! The worms are stampeding!'

'Waaaaahhhuuuuurrrrrrrgggggh!'

And every night, when they brushed their teeth together she would use toothpaste and he would use worms, and when he had finished he would make a point of spitting the sticky residue into the sink in front of her – a wriggling, wet lump of congealed strawberry bubble gum.

'Waaaaahhhuuuuurrrrrrrgggggh!'

***

For six years he tormented Evie. For six years her nerves lived on the edge. For six years his parents begged him to channel his love of worms into something positive.

'You could dress up in a long pink dress and do children's parties as Eustace the Worm Boy,' suggested his mother.

'Or write a worm recipe book for people who can't afford meat.'

'But I *like* teasing girls,' said Eustace, which explained why he regularly stood outside the ballet school trickling worms from his lips like dead man's dribble.

Then one day Evie snapped. It had been her birthday the day before and Eustace had brought her to the brink of hysteria by eating worm jelly in front of her friends. Angela Birkenstock was sick on the happy face biscuits, Phoebe Squall got as far as the chocolate éclairs on the other end of the table, and poor Scarlett Huckenbuck reached the door to the loo before re-tasting her breakfast. Evie's friends had run out en masse shrieking that never wanted to come to Evie's house again. Evie cried all night and the next morning was such an emotional wreck, that when she drank her orange juice and' found a clot of worms at the bottom of the glass, she freaked. She screamed so loudly as she ran into the garden that the glass in the back door cracked.

Mrs Colon put her head in her hands. 'The worms have taken over the asylum,' she groaned.

***

Evie was running round the garden in an uncontrolled way when next door's rather old and puffy dog came over to the fence to see what all the noise was about. It barked twice and caught Evie's eye. What she saw next brought her scream to a halt. It was a huge white worm hanging like a piece of string out of the dog's bottom! What could possibly be a better revenge?

Back in the kitchen, Mr Colon had reached the end of his tether.

'You're a disgrace to the name of Colon,' he fumed at Eustace. 'Go out there and apologise to your sister.'

'Why?' said Eustace. 'It's not my fault if she can't take a joke.'

'No,' said a flat, unemotional voice by the back door. 'It's mine.' Then to everyone's surprise Evie walked calmly through the kitchen and disappeared upstairs.

Mr Colon had still not finished making his point. 'Have you never heard of the expression "you are what you eat"?' he asked.

'Of course I have,' said Eustace. 'If I eat sprouts I'll grow a lot. If I eat peas someone will have to flush me down the toilet.'

'Don't be so rude,' said his mother. 'This is serious, Eustace. If you were to turn into a worm your life would be at an end.'

'Why?'

'Because you wouldn't have arms and legs, or eyes or ears or hair or taste or brains, and if you went outdoors the birds would eat you!' Eustace snorted with derision.

'Yeah, but it's not going to happen, is it?'

That all rather depended on what Evie did with the white worm. Had she known that it was a tapeworm – a worm that hooks itself into the guts of its host and feeds on the food in its stomach; a worm so greedy that it can even turn on the host itself — maybe she wouldn't have done what she did.

I like to think she would . . .

But she *didn't* know it was a tapeworm. All she knew was that it had come out of a dog's bottom. So she dropped it into Eustace's worm farm and went to ground till morning.

***

Twelve hours later, Eustace was woken by a knock on his door.

'Oh, Eustace,' came a cheery cry from the landing. 'I've brought you some breakfast in bed.'

He was confused. Evie never brought him breakfast in bed. In fact, Evie never came near him if she could help it. And now she was coming into his room.

'Get out!' he shouted.

'I just wanted to say sorry for screaming so loudly yesterday,' she said, placing a tray with a boiled egg and soldiers on the table next to his bed. 'I was wondering if we could call a truce? You know, I'm nice to you, so you're nice to me. Oh look, is that a new worm in your worm farm?' Being casual was all part of her plan. 'Ugh! It's big and fat and really disgusting!' She pretended to be horrified and turned away, knowing that Eustace would have to take a look. He was smitten. His eyes widened as he gazed on the white worm for the first time. It had eaten several of its pink cousins in the night and was bloated like a string of bloodless sausages. 'Oh, Eustace, no!' cried Evie, who had not gone through six years of hell without knowing the way her brother's mind worked. 'Please don't eat that horrible white worm in front of me or I'll be sick!'

Unable to resist, Eustace tipped back his head and lowered the overstuffed worm into his mouth until its head was dangling inside his stomach. Then he laughed and let it go.

Only this time, swallowing a worm did *not* have the desired effect. To Eustace's astonishment his sister did not scream.

'You don't know where that's been,' she smiled. 'But I do!'

Tapeworms are notoriously impatient creatures. Faced with a fresh body to plunder it got to work immediately hooking itself onto the stomach wall and ingesting all of the food it could find. Within minutes Eustace was starving and gobbled the boiled egg and soldiers. Then he went downstairs and polished off the contents of the fridge. Mr and Mrs Colon were delighted with the effect their chat had had on their son and congratulated themselves for weaning him off the worms, little realising that deep inside his belly a white tapeworm was gorging itself on the contents of their fridge before curling itself into the shape of a bomb and falling asleep in the outflow pipe of Eustace's stomach.

***

Two minutes after breakfast Eustace had a pain in his stomach. He lay on his front and kicked his legs in the air.

'Make the pain go away!' he cried. Evie mopped his brow with a wet dishcloth and made sympathetic noises so that her parents thought she cared. But she didn't.

Headaches are easier to cure than stomach aches. Instead of aspirin all you need's an axe. Gets the job done much quicker and it's permanent. As Petal can testify . . .

I'm the most loved little girl in the universe!

Not any more you're not. Petal.

After a lot of prodding, the doctor sent Eustace for an x-ray. When the pictures came back the problem was hideously clear for all to see. Curled up in his stomach was a tapeworm the size of a python. Even the doctor took a step back when he saw it.

'I have never seen one as big as that,' he said. 'I've heard of a tapeworm that size being found in Africa, but that was pulled out of an elephant.'

Eustace started to cry. 'I'm going to split, aren't I? It's going to keep getting bigger till I split down the middle!'

Evie was sitting quietly in a corner enjoying every minute of her brother's comeuppance. At the first sign of tears she jumped up and shouted, 'I know how to get rid of it. If the worm is in his stomach why don't we stick a harpoon up his bum and blow its brains out?' She was put outside into the corridor while the doctor outlined his prognosis.

'Not good, I'm afraid,' he said. 'That tapeworm is already too big for your stomach, Eustace. If it doesn't get a lot of food soon it's going to start to eat you, and if it starts to eat you, you're going to die, or, and I'm very much skipping around in the furthest fields of medical theory here, it's quite possible that it could eat your brain, not digest it and turn into you.'

'You mean my son will *become* a tapeworm!' gasped Mrs Colon.

'It's possible,' said the doctor. 'So I want you to watch out for any unusual signs like skin wrinkling, or eyelids gluing shut, or if, by accident, he should get cut in half, both halves of him leading independent lives.'

'What about my tongue turning white and filling up my mouth?' mumbled Eustace, parting his lips to show the doctor that it had already happened.

'Oh that's not your tongue,' said the doctor. 'That's the tip of the tapeworm's tail.'

Realising that they had to get some food into Eustace's belly fast to stop the tapeworm eating him, Mr and Mrs Colon rushed straight from the doctor's surgery to the supermarket. But in the car Eustace's hair fell out.

'Put your foot down!' shouted Mrs Colon. 'Or our son will be a worm before we get there.'

***

Eustace wasn't quite a worm when they pulled into the car park, but his arms and legs had started shrinking, his eyes were healing over and his waist had disappeared. Mr Colon picked up his son, threw him over his shoulder like a roll of carpet and ran into the supermarket.

'Gangway!' he shouted. But in his haste to reach the food, he misjudged the speed of the revolving doors and sliced off Eustace's back end. It was a gruesome sight. Shoppers screamed and ran around in circles as the back half of the boy plopped to the ground and wriggled around like a huge maggot.

'It's a boy who's a worm!' shouted the car park attendant.

'Freak!' shouted an elderly lady with a dog. 'Kill the freak!'

Within seconds, a mob of mad shoppers had formed, scared that whatever Eustace *had* might be catching. They wanted him dead.

'In the car!' shouted Mr Colon at his wife and daughter.

'What about Eustace's bottom half!' howled Mrs Colon. 'We can't leave half of him behind!'

'We have to!' ordered her husband. 'We can't save it now!'

He was right. The mob had fallen on the monster maggot and was beating it to death with their baskets.

As Mr Colon bundled his son into the car, three-and-twenty beak-licking blackbirds lined up on the telephone wire above his head, and when the car pulled out of the car park with all brakes squealing, the birds hopped into the sky.

The Colons only just got indoors before the mob came charging down the street chanting, 'Kill the freak! Kill the freak!' and brandishing garden spades and forks with which to chop Eustace up. They tore the gate off its hinges, trampled Mr Colon's roses, threw stones at the windows and thumped on the front door demanding that the human worm be sent out to die.

Mr and Mrs Colon were standing in the hall with Evie between them.

'Does everybody know what to do?' said Mr Colon. His wife nodded. Evie squeezed her father's hand. 'Then let them in,' he said.

When the front door opened the crowd fell silent.

'Can I help you?' asked Mrs Colon sweetly. When they told her what they were there to do, she reacted as if she didn't understand. 'You want to kill my son for being a worm!' she gasped. 'Surely there must be a mistake.'

'No! He's a devil!' shouted a woman's voice from the back of the crowd. 'I saw him cut in half and watched both halves live!'

'Well, you obviously know what you saw,' said Mrs Colon, playing her part to a tee, 'but my son is upstairs in bed with a cold and has been all day. If you'd like to see for yourself you're most welcome.'

**

The light was off in Eustace's bedroom when the mob entered. Had he not been wearing a woolly hat, scarf and pyjamas and had Mrs Colon not painted on a face with her make-up, the mob would have seen a white tapeworm sitting up in bed, but thanks to the disguise, it only saw a sick, pale-faced boy muffled up against the cold.

'Oh,' mumbled the shamefaced leader of the mob. 'There seems to have been a mistake here. Please, accept our sincere apologies.'

'No apology needed,' said Mr Colon. 'Mistakes happen. Think no more about it.'

'Even so,' said the leader, 'I do feel bad. I'd like to make it up to you before I go. I'm a doctor, you see . . .'

'He can't be examined!' yelped Mrs Colon, startling the doctor with her forcefulness.

'But we could open a window,' piped up Evie.

'Don't interfere,' snapped her mother.

'But opening a window will give Eustace some fresh air, and it might do him good.'

'The little girl's right,' said the doctor. 'Fresh air is nature's free medicine.'

'Oh,' said her mother.

'Right,' said her father.

'I'll do it,' said Evie. And while the mob quietly dispersed she opened the window like a good little nurse.

NURSE or MURDERER — the words are interchangeable, aren't they?

The following morning Mr and Mrs Colon were woken by a phone call from the police. A girl on a horse had found Eustace's pyjamas in a field three miles from the house and a window cleaner had discovered their son's hat on the roof of a public urinal. Mr and Mrs Colon dropped the phone, fell out of bed and rushed into Eustace's bedroom, only to find that the bed was empty. Three and twenty blackbirds had waited for the family to go to sleep before swooping through the open window and helping themselves to the largest worm supper they had ever seen.

And Evie never even shed a tear.

The shame for me was that I wanted Eustace alive so I could use him for fishing. Still, I'm making do with a Giant Moray Eel what I found hiding in my horn drawer. What I've done is hollowed out all the eel's guts and sewn a zip down the middle of its body, which has left me with a sort of fishy sock. Then when one of my SuperZeroes, one of my super little shipmates (it could be YOU), gets a bit above himself I zip him into the eel skin, attach him to a hook and fish with him instead.

Nothing's wasted down here. I collect the children's tears in a sealed bucket and feed them to the salt water crocodiles.

Now, some names are good, like Atilla, Vlad and Jaws. Some names, on the other hand, are a curse, like Rock, Chuck and Chip. People expect the owners of these names to be tough and rugged and make no allowance for the fact that they might be sensitive souls who like a good cry at a movie and aren't afraid to kiss their mothers in public. For girls, names such as Stinkypoo and Zittynose carry similar stigmas. People expect odours and spots and are shocked when they discover that the opposite is true. But the girl's name that carries the biggest stigma by far is Petal.

THE LITTLE FLOWER GIRL

When you think of a petal you think of something that is delicate and beautiful, soft, sublime and fluttery, fragrant and enticing. Imagine having to live up to that! Imagine having to enter a room knowing that, because of your name, you are expected to draw gasps of admiration from all those present. Petal Pansy Rose Stalewater was just such a girl. Unfortunately though, when Petal walked into a room, people did not see a vision in prettiness, they saw a snub-faced girl with no eyebrows, fat cheeks, thin lips, a crooked mouth and teeth like an untidy queue of white-suited Elvis impersonators in a Post Office. She was, in all respects, a perfectly ordinary girl to look at. She was not ugly, but she was no petal. This would not have mattered at all had she not been a girl with a dark obsession. She *wanted* those gasps of admiration from strangers and by hook or by crook she would get them!

Petal's insecurity stemmed from the fact that her parents never noticed her. They were always at work, which meant that every day when Petal got home from school she came in to an empty house. Actually, her parents weren't quite as negligent as that. They did pay the gardener an extra £54 a week to look after Petal until they got home from work, but Barker Grobag

A name which proves that sometimes people CAN get a name that suits them.

was a grumpy soul who detested children, because children sat on flowers. As a result of this, if Petal ever ventured into the garden he'd chase her out with his rake. She was always looking for ways to pay him back, so when he said gruffly one day, 'Tomorrow's Mother's Day. Don't even think of picking your mother some flowers!' she knew exactly what she had to do.

That night, she crept into the garden and picked a bunch of flowers. As it was dark and these were the first flowers she had ever picked, and because she was quite keen to upset Barker, she was rather clumsy and carelessly ripped the heads from the stems.

It worked. When Barker turned up for work in the morning and saw that twelve of his precious flowers had been brutally beheaded he watered the lawn with his tears. But something else happened as well. When Petal gave the flowers to her mother she smiled and threw her arms round Petal's neck.

'Oh, darling,' she cried. 'These are beautiful. What a clever girl.' And when she covered her daughter in kisses Petal thought she had gone to Heaven. This was the reception she'd always wanted when she walked into a room. For the first time in her life, Petal felt like she fitted her name and it was all thanks to flowers!

Whenever I have news to break to my guests down here on the SS *Pain and Eternal Torment*. I always like to say it with flowers if I can. YOU'RE FISH MEAT, SONNY JIM!

From that day on, Petal raided the garden whenever she saw an opportunity to make someone smile. She picked flowers for her teacher; flowers for the woman in the baker's and flowers for a passing dog. Flowers for milkmen, road sweepers, policepeople and lollipop ladies. Flowers for anyone, in fact, who'd give Petal a smile. And they all did. The only person who wasn't happy about the flowers was Barker, who eventually threw down his cap and resigned.

'Why?' gasped Mr Stalewater. 'Don't we pay you enough?'

'Have you seen the garden lately?' howled the gardener

'We're busy people,' said Mrs Stalewater. 'We're off before dawn and back after dark! When do we have time to look at the garden?'

'There are no flowers!'

'NO FLOWERS!' shrieked Mrs Stalewater. 'Where have they gone?'

'Ask Petal,' he growled, starting up the engine of his lawnmower, skidding across the pavement and chugging off down the road.

* * *

Petal's mother was grim-faced as Petal stood guiltily in the kitchen door. 'Barker tells me you've been getting your flowers from the garden,' she said crossly.

'Pretty flowers, Mummy. Picked with love.'

'Don't try and get round us with baby talk,' boomed Petal's father, storming in from the garden where he'd just seen the damage for himself. 'That's not picking, Petal, that's a massacre! It's like a battlefield out there.'

His daughter burst into tears. 'I wish I had a flower to give you, Daddy, and then you wouldn't shout at me.'

'Don't be so melodramatic, Petal. Now promise me that you will *never* pick flowers from our garden again!' Unable to promise, because her wobbly bottom lip prevented her from speaking, Petal nodded her head.

The idea of never being smiled at again, however, was just too awful to contemplate. She would pick flowers from *other people's* gardens instead, from parks and graveyards, roundabouts and allotments, from window boxes and baskets outside pubs.

'I'm SuperFlowerGirl!' she told her reflection that night before she went to bed. 'Bringing blooming happiness and love to the whole world with my pretty flowers!'

She also brought quite a lot of anger and hate. It was not long before the village was in uproar. Petal's neighbours were furious that their beautiful gardens looked so drab and bare and started a Neighbourhood Flower Watch. Groups of nature lovers kept an eye on their blooms with CCTV cameras and it wasn't long before SuperFlowerGirl was caught red handed outside the church tugging the head off a carnation in the middle of a bride's posy.

She was marched to the police station, thrown in a cell and the following morning was up in front of the judge. Her parents were too busy to attend, so she stood in the dock on her own with her right hand raised and her left hand resting on a Bible, promising to tell the truth, the whole truth and nothing but the truth. So much so that when Judge Ragwort asked Petal if she was ever going to steal again, she replied with total honesty, 'Yes, of course. I am going to keep picking flowers until I have picked the prettiest flower in the world and then I shall give it to you.' The judge was so surprised that his glasses fell off his face. 'It's called the Black Angel and I wish I had it now because then you would love me so much that you would definitely let me go.' But the judge didn't love her and sent her down for thirty days.

'To a place where there is no light!' he roared. 'A dark place where nothing ever grows, *especially* flowers!'

* * *

Petal didn't like her cell. It was *very* dark. She cried

out, but nobody came. In the morning one of the prison warders took pity on her tear-stained cheeks and called Judge Ragwort in his chambers. Still wearing his striped pyjamas and wig, he stumbled out of bed and came down to see what the fuss was about.

'It's five in the morning,' he grumbled. 'What's the problem?'

'I don't like it in here,' said Petal.

'You're not supposed to like it. You're a criminal.'

'Oh, boo hoo!' wept Petal. 'If only I'd had the Black Angel.'

'It wouldn't have made any difference,' he said. 'I can't let you out.'

'Yes, you can,' interrupted the kindly warder. 'What about the Grow Your Own Little Flower Girl?'

'The Grow Your Own Little Flower Girl!' exclaimed Petal. 'What's that?'

'Hush,' said the warder. 'The judge is thinking.'

First time for everything!

The Grow Your Own Little Flower Girl was a *Mark II Justice Doll* invented by Criminal Solutions plc. It was undergoing preliminary trials at the Home Office to see how effective it was at teaching bad children the difference between right and wrong.

It was a cross between Barbie and The Terminator

If Judge Ragwort was the first judge to sanction its use and it worked, he would go down in history as a great reformer.

'Very well,' he said, 'I shall change my judgement. I shall turn you over to the Grow Your Own Little Flower Girl and let her decide your fate. However it is my duty to warn you, Petal Pansy Rose Stalewater, that although this Little Flower Girl may be no bigger than a buttercup, she has the full force of the law behind her. What she says goes, so don't get any ideas about giving her the slip or treading on her head. Right, that's me back to bed.'

The judge left the cell in a cloud of peppermint breath-sweets as the warder handed Petal a tiny terracotta plant pot.

'Is this the Little Flower Girl?' asked Petal.

'Not yet,' said the warder. 'You've got to water her first.'

* * *

Five minutes later, a green shoot unfurled from the soil like the leg of a new-born spider. To begin with it grew straight up, but when it reached a height of five centimetres it twisted to the left, then back to the right, then up and down three or four times until it had sculpted itself into a tiny human skeleton. Then shimmering pink and white crystals put flesh on the bones and Petal recognised immediately what she had grown – a Little Flower Girl with the round yellow face and cross, black features of a pansy.

'You must be the criminal,' growled the Little Flower Girl as she stepped out of the pot and jumped onto Petal's hand. What Petal took for laziness in the Little Flower Girl's voice was in fact emotional detachment.

It is impossible to be an executioner without it.

'Right, I'm going to say this once and once only, so listen up. You belong to me. If you do as I say you will be released. If you don't, I am free to dispose of you any way I fancy. Is that clear?' Petal nodded. 'Good. Then here's the deal. We're going on a walk to a mountain in Wales. Along the way you will see flowers. Pick one and I will chop off a part of your body. When we arrive you will see The Black Angel. It is the only flower of its kind in existence. Pick that and I will chop off your head.'

'But it's the most beautiful flower in the world,' protested Petal. 'Anyone who sees it wants to own it.'

'Nobody said it would be easy,' said the Little Flower Girl. 'Now put me in your pocket and let's go!'

* * *

For the next three days Petal walked her socks off. She wore such big holes in them that she got blisters on her feet which popped and glued her skin to the inside of her shoes. The Little Flower Girl was a hard taskmistress. She refused to let Petal stop, even when she was tired, and took detours through fields of flowers to put Petal's powers of resistance to the test. When Petal weakened and her hand twitched because it wanted to pick a flower the Little Flower Girl would say in her cold, matter-of-fact tones. 'Pick just one flower and I'll cut off your ear!'

The first time she heard the Little Flower Girl say this, Petal was scared. The second time, when she heard, 'Pick just one flower and I'll cut off your toe!' she was scared again. But when she heard it for a third time, 'Pick just one flower and I'll cut off your finger!' a little bit of that fear had vanished.

'I'd like to see you try,' Petal said boldly. 'You haven't got a blade to cut them off with, and in case you haven't looked in a mirror recently, I'm nearly two metres high and you're "slightly" littler!'

'No bigger than a buttercup!' confirmed the Little Flower Girl.

'Precisely,' said Petal. 'So how you think you're going to cut off my finger without me squashing you first, I really don't know!'

'No,' said the cut-glass law-enforcer, 'you really *don't* know, do you?'

It was not being sure what the Little Flower Girl meant by this threat that kept Petal walking and stopped her from crushing the captor in her pocket; that, of course, and The Black Angel. If the prettiest flowers produced the biggest smiles, the owner of the prettiest flower in the world would be the most popular girl on the planet! This was Superflowergirl's moment to achieve immortality. All she had to do was steal the Black Angel.

I'M THE HOTTEST BOTTOM IN THE WEST!

Put it away. Bart. Nobody's impressed.

On the peak of Arenig Fawr, a circle of stones marked the spot where the Black Angel grew.

'We have reached the end of our quest,' said the Little Flower Girl. 'Sit down and drink-in the flower's beauty.' The petals of the Black Angel shimmered in the breeze like iridescent peacock feathers. They drew Petal's eye. They held her entranced and lured her towards it. 'You must look at it for one hour. If in that time you pick it I shall cut off your head. If you resist you are free to go. Understood?'

'But I don't want to look at it for an hour,' said Petal lifting the Little Flower Girl out of her pocket and setting her down on the ground.

'I am the law!' yelled the Little Flower Girl. 'You'll do as I say!'

'Not anymore,' smiled Petal. 'From now on we're doing things *my* way. And just in case you're still thinking of cutting my head off, I wouldn't bother. You'll never reach.'

'The flower is booby trapped,' said the crystal cop.

'Really?' sneered Petal. 'I don't believe you.' Then she lifted her right foot and stamped down hard on the Little Flower Girl's head. With a noise like breaking glass her crystal body shattered into a million twinkling shards which Petal kicked under a large rock. The Little Flower Girl was dead and buried. The Black Angel was Petal's for the taking.

Or so she thought . . .

She knelt down in front of the flower, stretched out her fist and closed her greedy fingers around the Black Angel's throat. The wind drew a breath. Then, with one fierce tug, Petal tore off the flower's head and stood up to admire it.

'You're mine now!' she cried. 'All mine! No …' The victory cry turned cold on her lips. 'What's happening?' The petals had turned brown and were dropping off the stem. 'NO!' she screamed. 'I FORBID YOU TO DIE ON ME!' but that was the least of her problems. Where there had been solid earth beneath her feet now there was only a sucking, squelching bog and she was sinking. This was the booby-trap which had been activated by plucking the flower. Petal was already buried up to her knees when her voice turned to panic. 'HELP!' she hollered into the void.

'I can help you,' replied a ghostly echo. 'Let me out before your arms are pinned to your sides and you can't help yourself.' Petal recognised the voice. It was the Little Flower

Girl calling out to her from underneath the rock. And she was right … Petal had already sunk to her waist. Another few seconds, her arms would be trapped and then she'd never pull herself out. 'Be quick,' urged the voice. 'Lift up the rock!' Petal pushed her shoulder forward and stretched out her hand. Then she stabbed the rock with her fingers until it rolled away.

The Little Flower Girl stood up and pulled herself together. Her cut-glass flesh reclothed her glittering bones and in her hand she now held a shining scythe. 'Oh dear,' she laughed. 'You didn't want to do that!'

A shiver of fear ran down the back of Petal's neck. 'If you're not going to help me,' she squealed as the bog slithered up to her chest, 'what are you going to do?'

'What I said I would do,' said the Little Flower Girl, 'if you picked the Black Angel. And now perhaps you can see why me being so little is not a problem.' Petal had stopped sinking. Just her head and neck were left exposed above the swamp.

'You can't cut off my head!' she cried.

'Why ever not? Isn't that what *you* do every time you pick a flower?'

Then the Little Flower Girl, who was no bigger than a buttercup, chopped off Petal's head with her crystal scythe, and the wind stopped and the clouds shed tears for the passing of the last Black Angel on earth.

Petal's head was rolled home by her assassin, partly to show Judge Ragwort that his sentence had been carried out, and partly as a warning to other little girls to not pick flowers to get friends. The Little Flower Girl stuck Petal's head on a bamboo stake in Mr and Mrs Stalewater's front garden, and there it sat for many a day. And many was the time that passers by, on noticing the yellow flesh and black sunken eyes, did remark upon its similarity to a pansy.

Of course she's down here now in the head waiter's cabin. That's the cabin for heads what is waiting to be used as cannonballs. There's a lot of nasty pirates in these waters what need repelling and there's nothing more repelling than a severed head with crabs scuttling in and out of its holes. Plus heads can see where they going so we never miss and some of the pirates are allergic to nuts. It's a positive slam-dunk!

Unlike every Grizzly Tale ever told this last tale does not have an avenging demon who exacts retribution on an evil child.

This is because the demon in this story is *INSIDE* the child a bit like that tapeworm. This SuperZero has no one to blame for his delicious demise but himself. The truth is this boy is stupid with a capital Loser, because he chose a life of crime and an early, if slightly bizarre death over a life of eating vegetables. He became the world's leading Supercriminal, the superest SuperZero of them all, hated and hunted by two billion people, just because he wouldn't stop playing poopy tunes. Every SuperZero has a nickname and Bart Thumper was known as The Evil Guff, because as you can probably guess, he had the most evil smelling guff in the world!

SUPERHEROES I WOULD LIKE TO SEE

No 112 – OdourGoneMan

Children are disgusting and cannot stop themselves from blowing toxic bubbles in the bath so imagine what it's like down here under all of this ocean – Bad Egg Bubble Central! So I want a Superhero who can absorb bad smells and squirt air freshener up my nose any time of day and night.

What did you say? You must have heard of The Evil Guff! The boy who held the world to ransom with his nuclear bum?

Fartypants
Fartypants
Too brown for party pants

THE RISE AND FALL OF THE EVIL GUFF

Even as a toddler, Bart was wilful. He was told to eat his vegetables and refused every time.

'I hate the colour green,' he said as soon as he could talk. 'Cabbage smells like elephant breath and sprouts are made of metal.'

'But they're good for you,' said his mother.

'Then I'll die, won't I?' replied Bart cheerfully. 'I've thought this through loads and I'd rather die than let a vegetable touch my lips!' Whenever he said this it reduced his parents to tears, which is why, of course, he said it. He never really thought he *would* die from eating vegetables.

So it must have come as a bit of a surprise when he did

It's just that there was a cruel streak to Bart even in the early days.

And so it was that throughout his early childhood Bart banned vegetables from the kitchen. It didn't stop Mr and Mrs Thumper trying to big-up vegetables in new and interesting ways. They wrapped them up for his birthday and gasped theatrically when he tore off the paper.

'Oh look, Daddy, it's a carrot!'

'You are *such* a lucky boy!'

They did puppet shows with green and yellow peppers, but Bart objected when the puppets turned up on his plate stuffed with rice and sultanas.

'I could *never* eat a vegetable that talked,' he said. They even invented a board game called VEG! in which vegetables took over the world and then got eaten, but Bart refused to play on account of it being unbelievable. 'Who's ever heard of a vegetable running the United States of America?' he snorted.

I can think of several . . .

Then on his ninth birthday, his parents got one over on him. By lacing his birthday cake with extra thick chocolate icing and a butterscotch filling that was so sweet it made Bart's teeth squeak, they managed to disguise the taste of a floret of cauliflower. They mashed it and liquidised it into a grey dribble which they then dyed brown and injected into the sponge. Bart was so excited by the party that he forgot to be suspicious of the large slice of cake on his plate and gobbled it down, only realising what he'd done when he saw his parents' beaming faces.

'There was something in that, wasn't there?' he screamed, sweeping the jam tarts off the table in a rush of temper.

'Your first vegetable!' his parents cried joyfully, not realising what they had just started.

Had Bart been a normal boy without terrorist tendencies they would have started nothing, but he was a boy who bore grudges. Its sounds incredible, but by lacing his cake with cauliflower Mr and Mrs Thumper put the future of the entire planet at risk.

**

After smashing the plate, Bart stormed up to his bedroom muttering dark words like 'betrayal' and 'revenge!' He tried in vain to think of a payback for

his parents, but nothing sprang to mind, until four hours later, when the liquidised cauliflower finally worked its way through his system, a tiny squeak from a hitherto silent place opened Bart's eyes.

'Is there a mouse in here?' he asked the

room. A second squeak, slightly warmer than the first, released another puff of wind into his trousers. Bizarre though it may seem, he had no experience of breaking wind and therefore no idea what was happening to him. He thought he'd sprung a leak and was just about to go downstairs for a puncture repair kit when a smell wafted up his nostrils. His first reaction was to panic, thinking his insides were rotting. Then in amongst all the other malodours he recognised the unmistakable stink of cooking cauliflower and made the connection. The first time in his life that he had broken warm smelly wind happened hours after he had eaten his first vegetable. Therefore vegetables caused warm smelly winds.

Now most of us are simply amused by our first smelly jelly, only a Supervillain like Bart could think of it as a weapon. Sensing that he had no more than a bubble of pongy gas left in his guts he ran downstairs to test a theory. His parents were in the sitting room watching telly when he strolled in.

'I hope you've come downstairs to apologise,' said his father. 'We had to send all your friends home.'

'Sorry,' lied Bart. Having manoeuvred himself near the sofa he clenched his buttocks and squeezed out the last bubble of sulphorous stink. His parents' reaction was loud and instantaneous.

'*Phwaaaaaaaaw!*'

They leapt screaming from the sofa as if they'd been stung by a swarm of bees, jumped over the coffee table, bounced off the wall and collapsed in a heap on the hearth rug.

'No more!' they shouted. 'We'll give you anything you want, just don't drop another one!'

It's vital that you understand just how smelly Bart's whootzie was. Imagine if you can a bucket of vomit, mixed with house fly pupae and mouldy blue cheese, rolled in armpits, squirted with essence of skunk, basted with cat pee, covered in the rotten corpse of a dead badger and owned by a sweaty darts player, whose hobbies include collecting bad crocodile eggs and storing fish in his pockets. Then add two tons of sour milk, a rotten cabbage, four dog blankets and a muck spreader containing the muck of six hundred and forty-three cows. Now double it and swill the mixture round in the bottom of a budgie cage … it smelled something like that.

Bart had just discovered that inside his gut he had the means to control his parents. He could get them to do what he wanted simply by threatening to guff on them. But first he needed fuel for his farts.

'You want us to buy WHAT?!' gasped his startled mother.

'Vegetables,' said Bart. 'You and Daddy were right all along. I do love vegetables after all.'

It was too easy. His parents thought they were doing right by buying Bart vegetables little realising that they were signing their own death warrants.

'VEGETABLES!' exclaimed his father.

'You know,' said Bart. 'Carrots, peas, sprouts, cabbage … You must know vegetables. They grow in the ground. Feed me!'

His parents were so happy that they fell into each other's arms and failed to notice the smirk on their sneaky son's face.

***

For one whole week Bart stocked up his gut tanks with gassy greens and bubbling Brassicas. On the seventh morning, the vegetables in his stomach had rotted into the most noxious gas ever smelled by man

Or skunk

and he was ready to change the balance of power.

He dropped his second bombshell in the car on the way to school. 'I don't want to go to school today,' he said to his father.

'Don't be silly, Bart,' came the automatic

reply, 'you have to.'

'No, I don't,' he said, 'because if you try to make me, I'll blow a bottom burp. Oops there it goes.'

Bart couldn't help himself. So rancid was the stink from his trouser trumpet that Mr Thumper was left gasping for air. Without checking in his mirror or indicating to the left he swerved across the road, bumped up onto the pavement and kicked open the door, only to come nose to nose with a red-faced policeman.

'You just ran over my foot,' he said. 'Out the car.'

***

The next day Bart got off school by targeting his teacher, Mr Deathbreath. In the middle of a maths lesson he yawned and called out, 'Stop.'

The teacher looked round in astonishment. 'What do you mean by interrupting me, boy?'

'I want to go home,' said Bart. 'I'm bored.'

'Nobody goes home till I tell them to,' growled the teacher.

'OK,' said the boy, bending over. 'Say hello to a pants puffer.' Then he tooted a hearty rendition of *Boomshackalak* out of his bumpipe. The stink caused violent vomiting in so many children that the

Environmental Health Officer was called in to check out the cleanliness of the kitchen and the school was closed down for a week.

And later that afternoon, when his mother took him shopping against his will, Bart told her to take him home.

'Or they'll be trouble,' he said. But she wouldn't listen. So he squeaked out a wet-one in front of the delicatessen counter. The moist heat from this gut-grinder buckled the shelves from Aisle 3 (Jams and Condiments) to Aisle 13 (Fresh Fish and Capers) before melting the plate glass windows. A green stink cloud escaped onto the street, causing concrete lampposts to wilt, paving slabs to curl like stale sandwiches and fire hydrants to burst. The buses were cancelled and Bart and his mother had to walk home. 'And let that be a lesson to you,' said Bart when they reached the front door. 'From now on, you do as I say, or pay the consequences.'

That night, after watching their smelly son on the TV news, where Chief Inspector Blair nicknamed him 'The Evil Guff' and described him as, 'dangerous and not to be approached,' Mr and Mrs Thumper dug out a pair of old gas masks from the cellar and rushed Bart to an all-night surgery at their local health centre. As luck would have it, the doctor on duty had specialised in Unsociable Wind at University College London and after measuring the strength and potency of Bart's rippers with a Canary test, he delivered his prognosis.

'It's not good,' he said, scraping the dead canary into the dustbin. 'Your son is a human stink bomb. He would appear to have an enlarged composting mechanism in his stomach which turns everything he eats into truckloads of methane.'

'Is there a cure?' asked Mrs Thumper.

'You could try sewing his bottom up,' laughed the doctor. 'Alternatively, he has to stop eating vegetables.' Eight days earlier, Bart would have met such a statement with yelps of joy. Not any more. Now that his eyes had been opened to the evil potential of his bowels he wanted more.

'WHAT?!' he howled. 'NO MORE EATING VEGETABLES!' The doctor stood up and leaned across his desk.

'For the sake of the planet,' he urged. 'It's only a matter of times before your emissions burn a large and irreversible hole in the ozone layer.' Bart's reply was succinct and to the point. He bent over and delivered a booming bubbler right up the doctor's nose.

***

When they got home, Mr and Mrs Thumper trussed their son up in a Clingfilm nappy and told him which way the wind was blowing.

'No more vegetables for you,' said his tearful mother.

'Then I'll find another source of fuel for my farts,' he said. His father dropped to his knees and begged Bart to reconsider.

'We'll do anything you ask, Bart. We'll raise your pocket money, buy you that table top map of the world that you wanted, even build you an indoor shark pool, but please, no more wind.'

'It's like living with a cow,' blubbed Mrs Thumper.

'A cow?' smiled Bart. 'Now there's a good idea.' Cows' creepers did more damage to the ozone layer than all the cars in the world put together. And what did cows eat? Grass! Which was why when Mrs Chuter, Bart's neighbour, happened to look out of her bedroom window at three o'clock the following morning, she saw Bart on all fours eating his father's lawn.

The grass accelerated Bart's decline into 'winanity'.

Which, as everyone knows, is insanity brought on by an excess of wind.

***

By nine o'clock the full and terrible effect of the midnight grass feast was unleashed on the world. If vegetables made Bart's flutterblasters smelly, grass added the nuclear factor. For the sin of passing the marmalade too slowly, Bart dropped a sly one in his mother's face and was taken by surprise when it exploded from his bum with the power of a tornado. The gale force wind blew his mother backwards across the table. She tried to anchor herself by grabbing onto Mr Thumper's jumper, but only succeeded in uprooting him from his chair and dragging him through the window with her. They flew across the garden fence and landed six miles away in the middle of a busy ring road, where a passing llama truck made pet food out of their heads.

To say that this was an unexpected turn of events would be an understatement. The last thing Bart had intended to do was kill his parents and turn himself into an orphan. Standing there in the kitchen, however, staring out at the world through the smashed window, he examined his feelings and discovered that far from being upset, he was actually *pleased*. The demon inside had taken hold. He had become 'The Evil Guff' There was nobody who could stop him now. By the power of his own phewies he was free at last to do EXACTLY as he wanted!

The police tried to catch him, the army tried to catch him, even secret agents tried to sneak up and catch him unawares, but he blew them all away. Anything with a nose and a sense of smell was no match for The Evil Guff, and as human beings they were just too light and insignificant to withstand the force of his nuclear bum blast.

The Prime Minister recalled Parliament for an emergency debate on the crisis, but even the politicians who were experts in the manufacture of hot air could not come up with a solution.

'Why don't we lock the boy up in a vacuum-sealed cell?' proposed a fresh-faced MP from the Mumbles. The House dismissed his suggestion with raucous laughter.

'In future, the right honourable gentleman would do well to put his brain in gear before opening his mouth,' said the Prime Minister with a smirk across his face. 'There is not a prison in this land can hold the Evil Guff. He's like the big bad wolf, Mr Speaker. He'll just huff and puff and blow the walls down.'

'So what can we do with him?' shouted the opposition benches. 'Let's have a policy!'

'Very well,' said the Prime Minister, searching for the first answer to come into his head. 'Bears!'

'Bears!' exclaimed the House.

'We make him live with bears.'

'Hear, hear!' cheered the Prime Minister's party. 'Excellent idea.' Anything their leader said was always a good idea, because if they disagreed he could sack them.

So bears it was. Bart placed behind a sixty-foot fence in the bear enclosure of Wetwipe on the Mould Zoo. The press turned out in their thousands to hear the Prime Minister announce that he alone was responsible for saving the nation from Bart's crunchy frogs.

'I don't get it,' shouted a journalist. 'What is to

stop the boy from dropping a big one while he's inside the enclosure?'

'Oh dear me, how little you know of bears,' chuckled the Prime Minister. 'Bears are not humans. They're naturally smelly creatures and will therefore be less offended by any seepage from the boy's cheesy colon.'

'But how will that save *us*?' persisted the hack.

'I'm coming to that,' said the Prime Minister sharply. 'Bears are also stronger than human beings and are able to withstand the full impact of a mega-guff without dying.'

'You still haven't answered my question, Prime Minister. Have you thought this policy through, or is it just another piece of hurried thinking thrown together to keep the voters happy?'

'Not at all,' came the tight-lipped reply, 'because if we're lucky, there's a good chance one of the bears might rip off the boy's head and play basketball with it.'

So *that* was the plan. The Prime Minister was hoping that a bear would kill Bart before he killed everyone else, but the truth was that the Prime Minister knew NOTHING about bears.

***

Mr and Mrs Bear were a sensitive couple who took pride in the cleanliness of their cave and believed in abiding by a strict moral code that involved daily exercises on the rubber ring and a cold bath before breakfast. Within minutes of Bart arriving and Mrs Bear getting a down-wind whiff of his pants Mr Bear felt impelled to pin the boy down with a paw and speak his mind.

'If we went outside and broke wind in front of our public all day,' he said, 'do you think people would still come to see us? No they would not. We have learned to control ourselves, Master Thumper. There is a time and a place for everything.'

'And the time is now!' sneered the revolting little boy who wouldn't be told what to do. Then he turned round and unleashed hell from his backside. But when he peered through his legs, expecting to see the bears splattered across the back wall of their cave, he got the shock of his life. The bears hadn't moved an inch. 'Right,' said Mr Bear. 'Now you've asked for it.' Then he and Mrs Bear sat right down and wrote the Prime Minister a letter.

DECEMBER 12TH

THE PRIME MINISTER
10, DOWNING STREET
LONDON
ENGLAND

DEAR SIR,

YOU INSULT US. FROM WHENCE DID YOU GET THE IMPRESSION THAT BEARS ARE COMFORTABLE WITH THE PRACTICE OF BREAKING WIND? HAD YOU EVER WATCHED ONE OF THE MANY TELEVISION DOCUMENTARIES MADE ABOUT OUR SPECIES YOU WOULD KNOW THAT WHEN WE BEARS HIBERNATE WE ARE SO MINDFUL OF OUR NEIGHBOURS THAT WE INSERT A TAPPEN IN OUR RECTUMS TO STOP THE ANTS GETTING IN AND NASTY SMELLS GETTING OUT. THIS BOY PONGS WORSE THAN A MEDIAEVAL MIDDEN AND WE SHOULD BE GRATEFUL IF YOU WOULD DESIST FROM DUMPING YOUR TOXIC PROBLEMS ON OUR DOORSTEP. UNLESS BART THUMPER

HAS DISAPPEARED FROM OUR LIVES IN TWENTY-FOUR HOURS MY WIFE AND I SHALL GO ON STRIKE AND REFUSE TO MEET THE PUBLIC. FURTHERMORE WE SHALL NOT ONLY CONSTRUCT AND PAINT A SERIES OF BANNERS ACCUSING YOU OF CRUELTY TO DUMB ANIMALS, BUT WE SHALL ALSO SEND A COPY OF THIS LETTER TO THE EDITOR OF THE BROWN BEAR TIMES AND IF THAT DOESN'T WRECK YOUR CHANCES OF EVER BECOMING PRIME MINISTER AGAIN THEN MY UNCLE'S A DUTCH MONKEY.

YOURS, ETC, ETC

PS FOR THOSE AMONGST YOUR GOVERNMENT WHO ARE IGNORANT OF THE ENGLISH LANGUAGE (MORE THAN SEVERAL, I FEAR) LET ME SAVE YOU THE TROUBLE OF REACHING FOR YOUR DICTIONARIES. A MIDDEN IS A LARGE DUNGHILL OR VAST STINKING REFUSE HEAP NEAR A DWELLING IN WHICH ORGANIC MATTER FERMENTS AND COMPOSTS INTO A NOXIOUS STENCH CLOUD; AND MEDIAEVAL MEANS OF OR IN THE STYLE OF THE MIDDLE AGES, A PERIOD OF UNPARALLELED FILTH AND SQUALOR BETWEEN THE 5TH AND 15TH CENTURIES.

***

For some inexplicable reason the bears were shot dead two hours after this letter was delivered to No 10 Downing Street, and the finger on the trigger reputedly belonged to the Prime Minister himself. But Bart Thumper escaped. As the Prime Minister swung his telescopic sight off the dead bears and realigned it with Bart's head, The Evil Guff stuffed his face with grass and used a high-pressure thunder-dumpling to propel himself over the perimeter fence.

He holed up in a cave in the Chiltern Hills and talked to the walls while the 'winanity' took over. His body was in such a wretched state from eating nothing but grass for months and his brain was so frazzled from lack of protein that he thought he was a strong, powerful bear who could stand up to smoofers. He could do anything he wanted and to prove it he issued a threat against the world. He recorded a broadcast from his cave and sent it to every television and radio station on the planet.

'Hello,' he said, looking directly into the camera with a wild-eyed intensity. 'This is The Evil Guff here. My needs are small, but your danger is huge, so tell your leaders to do as I say. Shout at them.

Throw stones at their heads if you must, but make them see sense. Unless I receive six billion pounds in used notes, a large house on an island with a cook who's good at making spaghetti bolognaise, a shark tank, a jet ski, a white fluffy cat and a table-top map of the world, I shall eat a whole field of grass and do such a big butt mutt that I will destroy the ozone layer in one go. Then all of you will be cooked up for good. You have one hour to accede to my request. Goodbye.'

***

Telephones rang across continents as world leaders hurriedly consulted each other about the best course of action to take. Meanwhile priceless art collections were carried down to sealed cellars; sunshade sales went through the roof; strangers kissed on trains; football matches were abandoned as a draw; workmen downed tools; insect leaders issued press releases that the world would soon be theirs; shops were looted; cars were crashed; submarines dived; people ran screaming from buildings; twenty-five billion bottles of champagne were drunk; and the Spice Girls urged everyone to go out and buy their new album. Then, fifty-five minutes later, the president of the United States of America delivered the world's reply.

'We do not negotiate with terrorists.'

***

And this was when it all went wrong. Believing that he had the power in his bowels to make the earth pay, Bart Thumper ate a field full of grass and assumed the position with his bottom poking out the entrance to the cave.

'I am the Evil Guff!' he cried. 'And I will be have what I want!' Then he relaxed his stomach muscles and let rip with a nuclear nwonk the like of which had never been seen or heard before. It was so powerful in fact that it blew a hole not in the ozone layer, which it passed straight through, but in the space-time continuum *behind* the ozone layer. And as everyone who's ever read a book knows, a hole in the fabric of time produces a suck twenty-eight trillion times more powerful than a Dyson Cyclone. Bart took off like a speck of dust off a carpet and shot through the hole in the space-time continuum into a Time Tunnel. His eyeballs liquefied in their sockets as his molecules were re-arranged then put back together again just in time for him to be spat out the other end. He hurtled out of a cloudy sky and plummeted to earth like an astronaut without a rocket, landing headfirst in a festering, rotten stench-pit of stinking crud and mire that was none other than a Mediaeval midden. In fact, he landed so hard that he was buried under fifty tones of Mediaeval crap, which meant that he was trapped. And over the next three years (from 1261 to 1264) he was slowly, ever so slowly, composted to death.

And if that's not a lesson on the perils of cutting the cheese in public I don't know what is! Apart from the unwanted bodily intrusion of a red hot poker, of course, which as well as being an effective deterrent is also a whole heap of fun!

Well, looks like you're staying after all. I've just received this letter from your parents.

DEAR CAPTAIN NIGHT-NIGHT PORTER,

RE - OUR SON/DAUGHTER (INSERT NAME)

WE'VE BEEN THINKING A LOT ABOUT OUR SON/DAUGHTER (INSERT NAME
_____) AS WE ALWAYS DO, BECAUSE WE MADE HIM/HER, AND
HAVE DECIDED THAT THEY DO ALWAYS THINK THEY ARE BETTER THAN
EVERYONE ELSE AT EVERYTHING AND SO WOULD LIKE THAT KICKED OUT OF
THEM IF YOU'D BE SO KIND. PLEASE GIVE OUR SON/DAUGHTER (INSERT
NAME _____) A CABIN AT NO CHARGE AND KEEP OUR
SON/DAUGHTER (INSERT NAME) LOCKED UP FOR AS LONG AS IT TAKES TO
CURE HIM/HER OF BEING A SUPERZERO. WE THINK YOU ARE THE NICEST
PERSON WE HAVE NEVER MET AND ARE DELIGHTED TO LEAVE THE
TREATMENT OF OUR SON/DAUGHTER (INSERT NAME _____)
UP TO YOU BUT WOULD LIKE TO POINT OUT THAT WHEN OUR SON/DAUGHTER
(INSERT NAME _____)CRIES OUT AND SAYS THINGS LIKE
'STOP! THAT'S HURTING!' AND 'I WANT MY MUMMY!' YOU SHOULD IGNORE
THIS, BECAUSE IT'S JUST ATTENTION-SEEKING, AND OUR SON/DAUGHTER
(INSERT NAME _____) HAS BEEN DOING THIS ANNOYING
THING SINCE HE/SHE WAS A BABY (CRYING, I MEAN). I HAVE ENCLOSED OUR
SON/DAUGHTER (INSERT NAME _____)'S PASSPORT IN CASE
YOU WANT TO GO ON HOLIDAY TO HADES.
THANKS A LOT FOR GETTING RID OF A REALLY BIG BURDEN IN OUR LIVES
LOVE
OUR SON/DAUGHTER (INSERT NAME _____)'S MUMMY AND
DADDY

PS THIS LETTER HAS NOT BEEN WRITTEN BY CAPTAIN NIGHT-NIGHT
PORTER PRETENDING TO BE YOUR MUMMY AND DADDY. TRUST US, OUR
SON/DAUGHTER (INSERT NAME _____), WE THINK HE'S
REALLY NICE AND YOU SHOULD DO AS HE SAYS.

PPS YOUR PET (INSERT NAME OF PET CAT, HAMSTER, RABBIT,
BUDGIE, DOG OR PONY _____) IS DEAD, SO THERE'S
NOTHING TO COME BACK FOR. GOODBYE, DARLING.

So that's settled. I'll put you in a cabin with all the other cruisers. You'll get a hammock, fashioned from the pleated throat folds of a Blue Whale, a potty hammered out of a sea urchin and an SS Pain and Everlasting Torment Welcome Pack. In addition to tea, coffee and soggy shortbread, there's an umbrella for unseasonably wet weather, a tube of Anti-Octopus Cream (Extra Slippy) to stop an octopus from hugging you, and a pair of lead-lined diving boots which guests are respectfully asked to wear at all times. Should you take them off in an attempt to escape, a day-glo T-Shirt emblazoned with the message FAST FOOD – PLEASE EAT ME and infused with the blood of a freshly slaughtered goat will be deployed over your upper torso to attract the man-eating sharks. Rest assured, we've thought of everything!

So here are your boots.

Where are you going? Don't 'Up up and away!' me when I'm still writing a book for you!